MW01234241

GREGORY A. SALLEE

MURDER
AT THE
HOUSE
IN THE
MIDDLE

novum ◢ premium

www.novumpublishing.com

© 2020 novum publishing

ISBN 978-1-64268-161-1
Editing: Karen Simmering
Cover photos:
Vectorshots, Juan Moyano,
Mikael Damkier | Dreamstime.com,
Gregory A. Sallee
Cover design, layout & typesetting:
novum publishing

www.novumpublishing.com

DEDICATION

I would like to dedicate this book to my family who gave me undying support during my time writing this book. Especially to my mother, Sharon Parker, my uncle Paul Patterson and my sister Lisa Taylor, all who wouldn't let me give up on myself and my dream of writing a book. Finally, to the support of Jake my dog that lay on my lap for many hours while I wrote.

TUESDAY

The sky was gray with the smell of rain in the air. There was a storm coming, everyone knew it, but no one knew when it would start. Detective Tom James, blond and tall, at exactly six foot four, and wearing a gray suit walked up the path. Tom was a family man with a wife and two young kids. He had loved his wife since they were in high school together. He loved his family more than a dog loves his bone and was very protective of his time with his family, to the point that he was rarely late getting home. Tom worked hard to uncover the reasons behind the crime no matter how obscure the story was. In this process he would find the killer and be able to give more information to the victim's family about why they'd lost their loved one.

As he arrived, he noticed that the house was a modest two-story with a yellow exterior and brown shutters at the windows, situated between two other houses on the block. There was a path moving from the sidewalk to the front door that was lined with rose bushes on either side. One window showed into the living room and two on the second story. The yard was well kept too. As Detective James walked into the house, the smell of rain surrendered to the smell of death. The house was well kept. The living room looked as if it had just been cleaned. There was a couch under the window and a wooden coffee table in front of it. There were two end tables with a tall lamp on each one on either side of the couch. There was a chair in the corner with a floor lamp behind it and an ottoman in front of it. In other words, it was like millions of other American homes.

The kitchen was a different story; it looked a little more lived-in. There were a few dishes in the sink. The breakfast nook table was a small round wooden table with four chairs around it and a pile of what looked like a week's worth of mail. There were crumbs on the table as if someone had just finished

7

eating a meal. Broken glass on the floor lay in a pool of water mixed with what appeared to be blood. There was blood all over the kitchen, a bloody knife on the floor and a bloody trail leading out the back door, fading on the grass right before the back gate.

Detective Thomas James found Detective Turner in the kitchen saying, "How did you get here?"

Detective Mike Turner, a stocky man about five foot eleven inches tall and wearing a blue suit, was kneeling next to the body. He was looking over what appeared to be stab wounds made by the knife lying on the floor. Mike loved to eat, which showed with his extra padding. He was single but didn't go out a lot, living alone in an apartment. Mike was okay with being alone but was always on the lookout for someone to spend his life with. He didn't like others fussing over him and trying to get him a date. He figured that he would find the right person when the time was right. He was always looking for the truth in everything. Mike was best friends with his partner Tom James.

Detective Turner said, "I rode over with the coroner."

"What happened Saturday last night? Why did you cancel your date?

"I didn't feel like going, she wasn't my type."

"Who are you kidding? You don't have a type."

"I just don't like set ups."

"Okay, okay. What do we have here?"

"The victim's name is Kathy Jefferson. She is 21 years old and appears to have been home alone. It looks like she let the killer in; there isn't any forced entry. She appears to have been stabbed to death with the kitchen knife that is on the floor. The knife was taken from the butcher block on the counter.

"With all the blood all over the room, it looks like a frenzied attack. This could be a crime of passion," commented Detective James.

Mike asked the coroner, "What is the approximate time of death?"

Dr. Shonna Johnson answered, "Based on liver temperature it looks like it was Sunday between 1 and 5 in the afternoon."

The room had blood on the counter, cabinets, and in a big pool on the floor surrounding the victim. She was leaning up against the cabinet with her arms at her sides. Blood was splattered through her long blond hair, and her baby blue eyes were wide open, with a look of fear. She was wearing a blue tank top, tan shorts, and white sandals.

Detective James asked, "Who discovered the body?"

Turner responded, "She is right over there. Her name is Kaitlyn Thompson; she is the victim's best friend she is pretty upset."

A young woman in her early twenties with long black hair wearing a white T-shirt and blue jeans.

As Detective James walked over to her, he got out his pad of paper and a pen. Kait appeared to be nervous and scared.

"How are you holding up?"

"I don't understand what happened," she said, sobbing, "She was so happy. How could this happen to her? Do you think that this was random, or could he come back?"

"It's hard to say. My name is Tom. How did you know her?"

"We met in high school and we became close. She is my best friend."

The detective asked, "Do you know of anyone that would want to hurt her?"

"No, everyone liked her. No one would hurt her."

"Where are her parents?"

"They all went to the beach for two weeks, Kathy came back early because school started yesterday after spring break. I should call them," she said.

"Don't worry about it; we will call them. What were you doing here?"

"I came here looking for her because she wasn't in class yesterday or today and she didn't answer when I called so, I came over to see why she was missing school. I used the spare key that they keep in the plant on the front porch. When I came in, she was just sitting there. She looked terrified."

"Where were you on Sunday between 1 and 5 in the afternoon?"

"I was at home working on my paper."

Detective James asked, "Was there anyone else there that could corroborate your whereabouts?"

"Yes, my parents were home, downstairs."

"Thank you, we may contact you again."

"Yes, I want to help find this monster."

"What is your address?"

"52697 Hanover Street."

"And phone number?"

"(555) 555–2368."

Mike walked over to Tom and said, "I'm done with the body and it is headed to the morgue for the autopsy."

Tom said, "Let's head back to the station and see where we stand with what we have so far. Besides, we need to contact the parents. They are still on vacation."

Once in the unmarked car, the two detectives started to theorize about the case.

Thinking out loud, Tom mused, "I wonder if there was a boyfriend. It's hard to believe that a young woman that attractive wouldn't have a boyfriend."

Mike responded, "She could have had a fight with the friend that found her. Finding her would give her a good reason to be there. She could have killed her over the weekend, waited a few days and when no one found her she could have gone over and 'found her' then called 911."

Tom said, "Let's look into her alibi and see where she was at the time of death."

Mike stated, "Why don't we go to her parents' house now before she can talk to them?"

Tom said, "Sounds good to me."

They drove over to Kait Thompson's house to see her parents Rodger and Lucy Thompson. On the way, Tom got on the phone and called Kathy's parents. Susan answered the phone.

Susan answered, "Hello?"

"Hello, this is Detective James. I'm from the Hollow Brook Police Department. I have some bad news that I need to share with you. Are you alone or is there someone there with you?"

"My husband is here with me. What is it? Has our house been broken into?"

"Ma'am, please have a seat before I go on."

"Okay, I'm sitting down. Please tell me what is going on."

Her voice sounded like she was in shock. She could only imagine what the detective was going to say next.

"We found your daughter this morning in your kitchen."

"Oh my God, did something happen?"

Her voice was now shaking and quivering as she spoke.

"Yes, she was found dead on the floor. She had been stabbed to death."

"No, you have to be wrong. That couldn't have happened. We live in a safe neighborhood."

"I don't want to get into it over the phone. So, when you get back come straight down to the station and we will go over everything. You won't be able to go home; it is still a crime scene. I'm sorry for your loss."

"Thank you. We will be heading back right away. We should be there by 4 o'clock."

As they drove up to the Thompson house the street looked like any other street in suburbia. There was a group of kids playing basketball in a driveway a few doors down and a couple of kids riding their bikes in the street. The yard looked well kept. The grass appeared to have just been cut. There was a tree that provided shade for the yard and the front of the house. It was a two-story house painted blue with white trim with a purple front door. There were two windows upstairs, one of them by the tree, and one large window in the front of the house on the first floor. There was a 3-car garage attached to the front of the house.

When they got to the Thompsons' home, they walked up to the door and rang the doorbell. They heard footsteps and then the door opened. There stood a beautiful woman in her late fifties, about five foot six, with long black hair wearing a long flowing red dress.

"Hello, can I help you?"

Tom said, "Hello, Mrs. Thompson?"

"Yes, I am Lucy Thompson."

"I am Detective James, and this is Detective Turner. Can we ask you a few questions?"

"What is this about?"

Mike said, "We are just wondering if your daughter was home on Sunday between the hours of 1 to 5 pm?"

"Why, what does it matter if she was home or not?"

Mike said, "We are conducting an investigation and she may have been a witness."

Lucy responded like the strike of a rattlesnake to protect her child from anyone and everyone that posed as a threat to her.

"Why, do you think that she is involved? My daughter wouldn't be involved in anything illegal."

Tom said, "Well, we have to see if she could have seen anything and if she hasn't then maybe she knows of someone that might have been around to see something. Besides, she is the one who discovered Kathy's body."

"Oh my God. She is going to be upset. I'll give her a call."

"Could you wait just one minute and tell us if she was home?"

"Okay. Yes, she was. She was in her room all day studying."

"Which room is Kate's room? Is it the one at this front corner of the house?"

"Yes, why do you ask?"

"No reason. Thank you for your time."

Tom and Mike walked away as the door shut behind them.

Mike turned to Tom and asked, "Why did you ask which room hers is?"

"You didn't see it? There is a tree just made for climbing outside of her window. So, her alibi is a little shaky. She could have easily climbed out of the window and gone over to Kathy's house."

"That sounds like a possibility."

"Hey, let's get some lunch before heading back."

Mike responded, "Where do you want to get something to eat at?"

"I was thinking Chinese. Let's go to Ming Palace."

"Sounds good to me. I've been wanting Chinese lately. Why don't we get Chinese more often?"

The restaurant was in a strip mall containing a grocery store, liquor store, and several other small retail stores. They parked right in front of Ming Palace. It was decorated with the traditional Chinese décor. There was a small dining room with three booths lining each side of the dining room with two tables in the middle of the room. There were red vinyl seats and seat backs on the booths and metal chairs at the tables in the middle of the room. The air was filled with the aroma of chicken, beef, and pork searing in the kitchen. A waitress greeted them as they walked in. She was wearing a brown and red vertical striped blouse and black pants with white tennis shoes.

"Sit anywhere that you like, gentlemen," she said with a pleasant smile.

They sat down at one of the booths across from each other and the waitress walked over and handed them menus.

The waitress said, "My name is Jiayi and I will be taking care of you tonight. Can I get you something to drink?"

Tom stated, "That is an interesting name."

"It's Chinese. It means auspicious one."

"That is really interesting. I will have an iced tea."

Mike said, "I will have a Coke."

"I will be back in a few minutes to take your order."

Tom said, "Okay, thank you."

Tom and Mike studied their menus like they were studying for a test.

Jiayi came back to the table. "Do you know what you would like to have?"

Tom said, "Yes, I will have the orange chicken with fried rice."

"I would like to have the beef with broccoli and fried rice."

"That is a good choice," Jiayi responded with a smile. "I'll have that right out for you."

Mike stated, "I'm looking forward to this lunch. I have been craving Chinese food."

"You are always craving all food."

"True."

"That tree outside of Kait Thompson's room is really bothering me. I think that there is more going on than what she is telling us."

"Yeah, I know something is off."

"I'm hoping that those canvasing reports show us something new; otherwise we don't have any more leads to follow."

"Also, maybe her parents will have an idea of who would do this to her."

Tom said, "Yeah maybe."

When the waitress came back with the food, the air around the booth was filled with the smell of orange chicken, fried rice and beef with broccoli.

"Here we go. I hope that you gentlemen enjoy," Jiayi said with a flirtatious smile.

After a bite, Tom said, "I have to admit this is really good."

"Yeah it is. This sauce is really good and actually seasoned properly."

"Well, if it has to do with food, you would know."

Tom and Mike ate their lunch, barely saying a word as they enjoyed their food.

As they finished, Tom said, "That was delicious. We really should look through the canvasing reports as soon as we can and see if anything looks out of place."

Jiayi brought the check to the table.

"Just take care of this when you're ready."

Tom looked at the check and it said the cost was $32.58. They put $41 in the folder and gave it back to Jen.

"Okay, I will have the change back in a minute."

"Keep the change."

"Thank you. Have a good day."

Mike responded, "You too."

As they left the restaurant it started to rain, just a slight drizzle.

Mike started to yell at the other drivers. "Don't you know how to drive? I swear people forget how to drive as soon as it starts to rain."

"You know they can't hear you, right?"

"I know, but it makes me feel better."

"Yeah, but it hurts my ears when you yell in the car like that."

"I'm sorry. It's just that they frustrate me so bad. It's just a little rain."

"Would it be better if I drive?"

"Maybe it would. I will pull over up here and you can drive in this mess."

Mike pulled in the driveway of a gas station up under the awning. They got out and switched places, Tom getting into the driver's side and Mike into the passenger's side. Tom pulled out of the driveway and into traffic. They drove about ten blocks without saying a word.

Then Tom said, "I believe that the rain is getting worse. I have been steadily moving the wipers to go faster and now they are on constantly."

"Can you still see?"

"For now, but it is still getting worse. Have the parents gotten back yet?"

"They are due back in about an hour."

"Let's go back to the station and meet them there. I promised that we would be there to meet them. I don't want to keep them waiting."

Tom drove back to the station and got there at about the same time as a car drove up in the front. The station was on a busy street with well-kept grass and bushes in the front. The detectives walked in through the back door from the police parking lot. The lot was filled with marked and unmarked police cars, with a staircase leading into the building leading to the back door of the station. In front of the building the Jeffersons were arriving walking up to the main entrance to the station. They walked in to the station and up to the front counter. The room was filled with chairs in the waiting area with half a dozen people sitting in them waiting for various reasons. There was a front counter stretching across the back of the room with several officers sitting behind it including the desk sergeant.

The desk sergeant asked, "Can I help you?"

"Yes, my name is Paul Jefferson. We are looking for Detective James."

"Okay, I will let him know that you are here."

The desk sergeant called Detective James on the phone.

"Hello."

"There is someone by the name of Paul Jefferson here for you."

Tom said, "Okay, tell him that I will be right out."

Sergeant Gonzales turned to the Jeffersons and said, "He will be right out. Please have a seat."

The Jeffersons walked over and took a seat in the waiting area.

"Hello, you must be the Mr. and Mrs. Jefferson?"

"Yes, I'm Paul. You must be Detective James?"

"Yes, but you can call me Tom. Why don't we go to the back and talk?"

Tom led them toward the back of the building. As they walked toward the back, they saw lines of desks with computers on them, desk chairs behind them and office chairs next to them in a large room with smaller offices lining the sides of the room. They went back to one of the private rooms to talk. When they walked into the interview room there was a couch and a couple of chairs surrounding a single coffee table. They shut the doors.

"Please have a seat," Tom said in a calm voice. "Can I get you something to drink or eat?"

Susan reached for some tissue that was on the table, but the box was almost empty. Susan and Paul still seemed to be reeling from the shock of finding out that their daughter had been murdered.

"I couldn't eat right now," Susan exclaimed, "I still feel sick."

"I'm really sorry for your loss." Mike stated, "We would like to ask you a few questions about your daughter's relationships in her life."

Paul responded, "Yes but I don't see how we can help. Didn't someone break in?"

Tom said, "It looks like she let the person in that killed her; we think that she knew her killer."

Susan said, "Oh my God, I don't know of anyone that would hurt her. She is—I mean was—the sweetest person. She was liked by everyone."

"Well, someone wasn't happy with her."

"Anything that we can do to help?"

"Good, that's what we need. Is there anyone that either of you can think of that would want to hurt her?"

"No, not that I know of, but you know more of her friends than I do," Paul said, looking at his wife.

"I don't know of anyone."

Mike said, "It could be anything. Is there any chance that she was fighting with anyone?"

Susan said, "Well she did just break up with her boyfriend. I remember because she came to me and told me that I would be proud of her for ending it. I was always after her to end it because he is no good. But he kept coming around to try to get her to come back to him. I told her that I was happy that she had realized it for herself."

Mike whispered, "It's the boyfriend again."

Paul said, "What do you mean by that?"

"Well, it seems that the boyfriend keeps coming up." Mike affirmed, "What is his name?"

Susan interrupted, "His name is John Murphy. The last time that he was around was about a week and half ago. They were arguing about her dumping him and he wanted her back."

Tom asked, "Was there anybody else that she has been in any disagreements, with no matter how small?"

"Now that you mention it, she has been having an argument with her best friend Kait."

"Kait Thompson?"

"Yes, have you already talked to her?"

"Yes, she found Kathy's body, but she didn't say anything about an argument. Do you know what the argument was about?"

Susan said, "No, she wouldn't talk about it. I figured that she would talk to me about it when she was ready."

Tears started to run down her cheeks like Niagara Falls, as she quivered from being upset over losing her daughter. Mike passed a new box of tissue to Susan.

As she reached for it, her voice cracked as she cried, "I guess now I will never know."

Mike said, "We will do our best to get some answers for you."

Susan demanded as she slapped her hand down on the table, "You promise me that you will find her killer!"

"I won't make a promise that I can't guarantee," Mike exclaimed. "I will do this, I will promise that we will do everything that we can to figure this out and answer your questions."

"Why don't you two go get some rest and we will let you know when we find anything, okay?"

Paul responded, "Okay, let's head to the hotel. We will be staying at the Hilton in town."

"Okay we will be in touch."

As the Jeffersons left the building, Tom turned to Mike and declared, "Well, I'm going to go home to my wife and kids. I have a need to see my family."

"Yeah, it's a good time to take a break and look at it with fresh eyes in the morning."

As Tom drove, he anticipated getting home and hugging his children and kissing his wife. After the day that he'd had, he couldn't wait to be with his family. His family was a constant reminder to him that there is still good in the world. He used his family to ground him and allow him to still believe that there were people that were worth his effort to seek justice. Seeing his children reinforced his conviction that all victims needed justice and drove him to find the truth for victims' families. It wasn't just catching the killer; he needed to find the story and why the victim was killed. Without the story there would be no justice. Tom needed to find the story so that he could answer the question of why no matter how twisted the answer was. He felt this was the only way that the family could have the closure that they were carving. This would help them move on and still live a full life without living in the past.

As Tom drove up his calm and quiet street, there were cars in the driveways with lights on in the houses. Some houses had porch lights on; others were turned off. As he pulled into his driveway, he felt a since of calmness come over him.

"I am home," escaped his lips.

His house was a modest two-story, gray with tan trim. The front door was white, and there was a two-car garage attached to the front of the house with a red door. There were two trees in the yard that were as high as the house. He took pride in his yard, so the grass was well-kept, and the bushes were trimmed.

Arriving home, Tom walked through the door and his children came running into his arms. Wrapping his arms around them, Tom picked them up for a quick second and then set them back down.

With love in his voice, he said, "You both are getting so big. I swear you grew while I was at work today."

He entered the living room, where there was a couch dividing the living room from the dining room. There were two chairs with a table with a lamp coming out of the top between them. There were end tables on either side of the couch and a coffee table in front of it. There was a television opposite the couch at the other end of the room. The stairs came down behind the television. You could see the dining room with a wooden table and six wooden chairs around it with two on each side and one on either end.

The children were six and eight years old. His six-year-old, Jeremy, had blond hair and stood about three feet tall, wearing green pajamas. His eight-year-old, Anna, had long brown hair and stood about three and a half feet tall, wearing a blue nightgown. His children looked at their father like a hero.

His wife, a beautiful, tall woman named Karen, stood about five foot eight with long brown hair. She was wearing a colorful skirt with a white blouse. She walked into the room and kissed him hello. Karen started dating Tom in high school. She trusted him without reservation. She was proud to be a cop's wife and was very proud of who Tom was. She was a mother and housewife before anything else in her life. Her family was everything to her and she would do anything for them. Karen loved being a mother; it had always been her dream. She was thankful to Tom for helping her make that dream come true. She had made it her personal mission to find Mike a wife.

"You're late!" Karen scolded jovially. "You missed dinner. I saved you a plate."

"I know. I'm sorry that I didn't call," Tom responded. "Thank you. I was busy at work and I couldn't get away."

"What happened? I'll get you your plate."

"I was with the parents of a mur..."

"Wait, not in front of the kids."

"Sorry, I forgot that they were here."

Karen walked into the kitchen and came back with a hot plate with meatloaf, corn, and mashed potatoes and gravy, along with a cold beer to drink.

"Okay kids, you got to wait up for your dad, but now it's time for bed. I'll be up in a few minutes to tuck you in."

"Goodnight, Daddy! I love you!"

They ran up and gave him hugs and kisses.

"Goodnight! I love you too!"

The children started to run up the stairs and Karen yelled, "Don't forget to brush your teeth. I will be checking!"

"I'm sorry that I was late. I was waiting for the parents of a murder victim to come home from vacation. Their daughter came home early because school was starting."

Karen was used to her husband bringing home bad cases but there was something about this case that really hit too close to home for her. There was a similar situation when she was a kid and a neighbor a few doors down and around the corner was killed during a home invasion when she was growing up. This case brought back some bad memories of that time when she was in junior high school, about 12 years old.

"This reminds me of that neighbor that I had when I was a kid who was killed in a home invasion," Karen said, shaking with fear. "Do you remember me telling you about that when we first met in high school? Do you have any leads?"

Tom responded, "Yes we have two promising suspects that were having fights with her. The ex-boyfriend and the best friend both might have a motive, so we are going to check them out more tomorrow."

"I better go check on those kids and make sure that they are in bed."

Karen walked up the stairs to find the kids playing in their rooms. The wall next to the stairs had family pictures on it all the way up.

"You had better both be in bed before I get to your rooms."

She could hear them scrambling to get into bed. Karen walked into Anna's room first, which was filled with stuffed animals; there wasn't a corner without a stuffed animal in it. The walls were a light pink and there were Barbie dolls and Disney princesses all around the floor. She had a white twin bed with a white canopy.

"Anna did you brush your teeth?"

"Yes, Mommy, I did."

"Okay, goodnight."

She tucked in Anna and walked to the door and turned out the light. She headed to Jeremy's room, which was filled with stuffed animals and trucks with the occasional action figure on the floor. The walls were a light blue. He had a set of bunk beds where he slept on the bottom bunk with a blanket tucked under the top bunk, forming a little hideaway.

"Jeremy, did you brush your teeth?"

"Yes, Mommy I did."

"Okay. Goodnight."

Karen walked out of the door, turning off the light as she left the room. Then she paused at the bathroom and thought, I wonder? She walked into the bathroom and checked the toothbrushes. Anna's was wet, and Jeremy's wasn't.

"Jeremy, you had better get up and brush your teeth like you said that you did. Don't lie to me again!"

Jeremy got out of bed and ran into the bathroom. "You really do check, don't you?"

"Yes, I do! Now go back to bed. I love you both! Goodnight!"

The children said in unison, "I love you!"

Karen walked back downstairs to find her husband sitting in his chair.

"So where are you in the investigation?"

"Well, we are going to look into the ex-boyfriend tomorrow and see where he was when she was killed."

"You think that he had something to do with it?" Karen asked.

"Well, he was seen having an argument with her about a week ago. He seems to have trouble letting her go. It appears to be a crime of passion, so he has motive," Tom said, yawning. "Well, I'm tired so I'm going to go to bed."

"I'll be right behind you."

Tom went upstairs and changed clothes. He was getting into bed just as Karen came in. She quickly changed clothes and climbed into bed with her husband. Karen turned on the news to watch as she fell asleep.

WEDNESDAY

Tom woke up and walked downstairs to find his kids sitting at the table eating breakfast and Karen fixing him a plate of scrambled eggs with cheese, bacon, and toast with strawberry jelly. He sat down at the table with Jeremy and Anna. Karen walked over and put his breakfast in front of him.

"Thank you for this. You didn't have to."

"If I didn't you would have coffee and not eat, and you need to eat. Coffee?"

"Yes please."

Karen fixed herself a plate and sat down with her family. They ate and chatted about the coming day.

Tom asked, "So what do you kids have going on today?"

Anna said, "I have a math test today."

"We are working on writing our ABCs."

"Sounds like you guys are going to have a fun day."

"How is a math test fun?"

"Trust me, when you get older you will miss your time in school and growing up."

"I'll take your word for it."

They finished breakfast and the kids headed to the school bus, with Karen walking behind them to make sure that they made it there okay. She walked behind them to give them a sense of freedom. Tom headed for the door as well. By the time Tom got to the office, Mike was already there.

Tom said, "I want to go back and talk to Kait Thomson again."

"Why do you want to do that?"

"Well, that tree is bothering me. I want to ask her about it."

"Then let's go find out what she has to say about it."

Mike and Tom walked to the car in the parking lot at the back of the building and got in to head to Kait Thompson's house.

Mike said, "Do you really think that Miss Thompson is our killer?"

"No, I just think that she is hiding something. I believe she is holding something back from us."

"What do you think that is?"

"I think that she might know who the killer is, but maybe just doesn't know it yet."

"Yeah maybe," Mike pondered. "I guess it's easy to overlook something if you don't realize that it is relevant."

"That is exactly what I was thinking."

There was a short silence as they constructed questions to ask her. As they pulled up to the house, they gave each other uncomfortable looks. It was a delicate situation dealing with the person that found the body. They both knew that it would be easy to retraumatize her. They walked up to the house and knocked on the door. Richard Thompson answered it.

Richard said, "Can I help you?"

"Hello, I'm Detective James, and this is Detective Turner. We would like to ask Kait some more questions about Kathy Jefferson."

"I don't think that she is up for it. She just lost her best friend."

"And we are just trying to find a killer," Tom exclaimed. "The killer that killed her best friend."

"I just don't think …"

He was cut off by a voice coming from behind him.

Kait said, "Dad, I want to help in any way that I can."

"Okay, if that is what you want, sweetie. Come in and have a seat."

Mike said, "Thank you."

Mike and Tom walked in and saw a formal living room with a deep red couch under the window, and two metal and glass end tables on either end of the couch. There was a metal and glass coffee table in front of the couch. There were two white chairs opposite the couch with a wooden table in between them. Mike and Tom sat down on the couch and Kait walked in and sat down on one of the chairs. Her father, Richard, stood right by her.

Tom asked, "Is there anything else that you remember from yesterday?"

"I don't remember anything else that I haven't already told you."

"Well, is there anyone that you can think of that she was fighting with?"

"She was having a hard time with her ex-boyfriend."

Mike asked, "What do you mean?"

"She broke up with him, and he doesn't want to accept it. He keeps coming around uninvited."

"So, he is stalking her?"

"I guess so. She kept complaining that he was everywhere that she was, and she would think that she saw his truck in front of her house several times even at night, but she wasn't sure."

Tom asked, "How long were you in your room on Sunday?"

"I was in there all day, except to come out and get something to drink. Why?"

"Well, we saw that tree outside of your window and how easily it would have been able to sneak out without anyone knowing."

"I will tell you this. I have used that tree in the past, but I didn't use it on Sunday. Ever since I turned eighteen my parents have stopped monitoring where I go, so I haven't needed to sneak out. If I want to go somewhere, I just go."

"I thought about cutting it down when Kait was about sixteen but decided not to." Richard commented, "Now, there isn't any reason to. She is an adult and can go out whenever she wants."

Mike asked, "Why did you consider cutting it down?"

"Because she was climbing out of her window about every other weekend."

Mike handed her a card. "Here is my card. If there is anything else that you can think of, please give us a call. If we have any more questions we will be in touch."

They all stood up and walked to the door.

Richard opened the door. "Have a nice day."

Tom said, "You too. Thank you again."

"You're welcome."

Richard shut the door as Tom and Mike walked back to the car and got in to drive away.

Mike turned to Tom. "What do you think?"

"I believe her, but I think that she still might know something more."

"You think that she is still hiding something?"

"Hiding something or doesn't know that she knows it or both. We will just keep her on the back burner."

"That's a good idea. Hey, let's stop to get something to eat."

"There you go again. You can't miss a meal, can you?"

"No, I can't. It goes against everything that I believe in."

"I swear that you have a one-track mind."

Mike responded, "What can I say? I'm hungry!"

"Where do you want to go for lunch?"

"I don't care."

"It's up to you. You're the hungry one."

"Okay, let's go to a Mexican restaurant."

Tom asked, "Okay. How about Mi Casa Su Casa?"

"Sounds good."

They dove up to the restaurant and parked in the parking lot. The building was a free-standing building made of red brick with glass windows on three sides with a green metal roof. As they walked up, the smell of spices and caramelized onions wafted through the air. There was a hostess stand at the front of the restaurant, a dining room behind it and a bar off to the right. The dining room had booths to the left as you entered and tables to the right with wooden chairs. The room was colorful with bright yellows, greens, and reds. Upon walking into the restaurant, they were greeted by a hostess. She was wearing black pants with a yellow blouse with the restaurant logo on it and black tennis shoes.

"Is it just the two of you?"

Mike said, "Yeah, just us."

The hostess showed them to a booth on the left side of the room. Shortly after they sat down, a waiter walked over, wearing black pants, a red shirt with the restaurant logo on it, and black tennis shoes.

"Hello, my name is Steve. I will be taking care of you today. Can I get you something to drink?"

Mike said, "Yes, I will have a Coke."

"Please, I will have an iced tea. Thank you."

Steve disappeared and came back with the drinks.

"Do you know what you would like to eat?"

"Yes," Mike said anxiously, "I would like to have the seafood enchilada."

"I would like to have the fish tacos."

"Okay, I will get that in for you."

Mike said, "Thank you."

Steve walked away to turn in their order.

Tom said, "I think that I will run John Murphy's name through the system when we get back."

"I think that that is a good idea. He seems to be in the middle of all of this."

"If John Murphy did this then we should be able to figure this one out fast."

"But what about that window at Kait Thompson's house, by her bedroom?"

"That does still bother me."

When the food came the aroma filled the air and just made them hungrier.

Tom said, "Oh, here we go."

As their food was placed on the table, Steve remarked, "Be careful. The plates are hot."

Mike said, "Thank you."

"You're welcome. Is there anything else that I can get you?"

Tom said, "No, I think that we are fine for now, thank you."

Steve walked away to let them enjoy their lunch.

"Boy, this looks good. I love fish tacos."

"Mine looks good too."

They ate their lunch, all the while pondering who was this John Murphy. As they were finishing, Steve walked up, bringing them the check.

"Just take care of this when you're ready, there is no rush."

Mike looked at the check and it said the total was $33.68. He put $42 in the little folder. Then he signaled the waiter to come back.

"I'll bring you back the change."

"No need. Keep the change."

"Thank you. Have a wonderful day."

Tom said, "You too."

They walked back to the car and got in to head back to the station.

Tom said, "I think that we should go through the canvasing reports when we get back."

"That is a good idea. We might get another lead from those."

"Well, it looks like the best friend isn't going to work out as a suspect. But I still want to know what she is not telling us."

"Yeah, but it doesn't make since to not tell us everything if she wants us to find the killer."

"People hide things for all sorts of reasons. We just need to find out her reason."

"Well, we will figure it out."

"Yeah, we have to," Tom snapped. "This is one that I need to figure out."

"Why are you taking it so personally?"

"Because it was just so senseless. I need to get some answers for her parents."

"I can understand that," Mike pursed, "but it seems to be more than that."

"It goes back to before I met Karen. She had a neighbor get killed during a home invasion and they never found the killer. It still bothers her to this day."

When they got back to the office, they started looking through the canvasing reports.

Tom said, "Look at this. The neighbor next door said that he heard a scream, but he didn't hear anything else after that. He said that he heard the scream at around 3:30 pm on Sunday."

"Let's go back to the scene and talk to this guy and see if he knows anymore."

"Let's go."

Tom and Mike walked out to the car and started to drive to the crime scene.

"So, how is your family doing?"

"They are doing good. Anna is getting good grades at school and Jeremy is learning his ABCs and numbers."

"How is Karen doing? Has she thought about going back to work since both kids are in school?"

"She hasn't mentioned it lately, but I think that she wanted to get Jeremy into first grade before she did anything."

"That's probably a smart thing to do."

"Wow, we are here already."

When they got back to the scene the street was quiet. There weren't any children playing outside after school, even though it was a nice day. It was kind of eerie. It was a tree-lined street with branches stretching over the street which made it seem like the perfect neighborhood where nothing bad could ever happen. The houses were cookie cutter; every fourth one was identical. They headed to the neighbor's house, on the corner. The house's yard was immaculate; it had just been cut. There was a walkway going up through the middle of the yard lined with rose bushes on either side alternating red and white roses freshly pruned. The tree in the yard had been cut back with no dead branches on it.

The house was a two-story house with tan paint and dark brown trim. There were three smaller upstairs windows and one large one downstairs. There were mini blinds on every window pulled closed. The front door was red. There was a blue SUV parked in the driveway. There was a two-car garage in front. They walked up to the neighbor's house.

Mike said, "This guy's name is Todd Walker."

They knocked on the door and Mr. Walker answered it. He was a gangly man about six feet tall with brown hair, about 35 years old wearing blue jeans and a green T-shirt.

"What can I do for you?"

"I'm Detective James, and this is Detective Turner. We just have a few questions for you."

"I already told the cops that were here earlier everything that I know."

"This will just take a few minutes of your time," Mike exclaimed. "Is there anything else that you remember about Sunday afternoon?"

"No, there wasn't anything unusual that day."

Tom asked, "Were there any cars on the street that didn't belong? Did you see someone hanging around the house that didn't belong?"

"As a matter of fact, there was a white truck on the street that didn't live here. I believe that it belonged to her boyfriend. I remember that she was arguing with him the week before she left with her family for vacation."

Mike asked, "Do you know what they were arguing about?"

"No, but she was crying. It sounded like he was mad at her for something. He kept saying that she was making a mistake and she was going to ruin her life, and nobody will understand."

Tom asked, "What does he look like?"

"He is about five foot ten inches tall, brown hair cut in a buzz cut, and has tattoos all over his arms and neck."

"It sounds like you know a lot more than you said originally," Mike said. "Why were you listening so close to that argument? Were you a little more interested in her than you let on?"

"No! I just overheard them because they were so loud. I just remembered when you asked me."

Tom said, "Okay, thank you for your time. If we need more, we will be in touch. Have a good day."

Tom and Mike walked away from the door, satisfied that they had a new suspect to investigate. As they start to get in their car, Mike noticed an older woman watching them through the front window.

Mike said, "We should talk to her."

"Who?"

"That lady watching us through her window. A woman like that always knows what is going on in her neighborhood. There isn't much that gets past her."

"Well, let's go talk to her then."

They walked over to her house. They noticed that the grass needed to be cut, and the bushes were overgrown. There was a dead tree that looked like it should have been cut down years ago. The yard looked like it had not been tended to for at least a month. The house was a modest one-story house. It was painted a pale-yellow paint with white trim. There was one large window in front with white shutters. There was a two-car garage in front with a yellow door. The front door was white. As they approached the house, they saw her disappear from the window into the house. They knocked on the door and as it opened, they saw an older woman appear in the doorway. She was about sixty years old, about five foot five and was wearing a blue house coat and blue slippers. Her curly hair was gray, and she wore black-rimmed glasses.

"Hello. I am Detective James, and this is Detective Turner. Can we ask you a few questions?"

"I guess. Is this about what happened across the street?"

"Yes. What is your name?"

"My name is Gladys Baxendale."

Mike asked, "What do you remember about last Sunday afternoon?"

"There didn't seem to be anything unusual, but around 3:30 pm I heard a scream. I was indisposed at the time so as soon as I could I went to the window to see if I could see anything but there wasn't anything to see."

"Did you see anyone go into the house?"

"No, like I told you I was indisposed. I didn't see anyone come out either."

Tom asked, "Did you see anything on the street, like an unusual car or a truck?"

"No, I didn't see anything like that, but I wasn't able to come out right away, so I guess they could have left before I got to the window."

"Did you hear a car pull away before you got to the window?"

"No, I didn't, but I don't hear well anymore either."

"Did you see a white truck outside the house the week before they left for vacation?"

"Yes, there was. The young girl was arguing with a young man something fierce. That boy is trouble."

Mike asked, "Why do you think that he is trouble?"

"Well, he looks scary and has tattoos."

"Can you describe him?"

"Yes, he is medium height and medium build. He has short hair like a buzz cut and tattoos on his arms and neck."

Tom asked, "Do you know what they were arguing about?"

"No. Like I said I have bad hearing."

"Okay, thank you for your time. If we need anything else, we will contact you."

Gladys shut the door and Tom and Mike started to walk away.

Mike turned to Tom. "Well, that sort of verifies the story of the next-door neighbor."

"I think that we need to talk to that boyfriend."

"Let's head back to the station."

"I liked that lady. I'm just not sure how reliable of a witness she would be."

"She isn't quiet all there. Besides, I don't think that she saw enough to use her in a trial."

"Todd, on the other hand, seemed too eager to share what he has."

"We will have to keep an open mind when it comes to him."

"You know after all these suspects wouldn't it be a real kicker to find out that it wasn't any of them?"

"I think that we should just concentrate on the ones that we have in front of us for now."

"Well, we sure don't have a shortage of suspects. Shall we head home for the night and look at it with fresh eyes in the morning?"

When they got back to the station, Mike dropped Tom off at his car.

"That sounds like a good idea. Go ahead, I'll turn in the car. See you in the morning, Goodnight!"

"Goodnight!"

Tom drove home wondering if Anna had passed her test today and if Jeremy was able to finish his ABCs. The drive was relaxing but the day's clues kept occupying his mind. He couldn't help but think that something deeper was going on. As he drove up to his house all he could think about was going in and seeing his family after a long day.

Tom walked into the house and hollered, "Is there anybody home?"

Karen yelled back, "We are in the kitchen."

Tom walked into the kitchen to find his kids sitting at the table working on homework and Karen was in the kitchen working on dinner.

"Hey, Anna, how did you do on your math test?"

"I got a B minus."

"That's good. A B is good. I'm proud of you. Hey, Jeremy, how are your ABCs coming?"

"I almost got them. I have to write them 5 times tonight for homework."

"Karen, what's for dinner?"

Karen responded as she pounded out chicken breasts, "We are having Chicken Kiev, baked potatoes, and green beans."

"Wow, fancy. What's the occasion?"

"I just wanted a nice dinner."

"Well, is there something that I can do to help?"

"Yes, you can finish pounding out these breasts while I get the onion chopped."

"Okay."

He walked around the counter as he rolled up his sleeves and then washed his hands. Tom reached for the mallet and smashed it repeatedly down on the chicken breast.

"Karen, how was your day?"

"Well, I had a multitude of errands to run today. You know: store, dry cleaners, lunch with Allison and our adorable son forgot his lunch today so I had to run that over to him."

Tom and Karen finished making dinner. While the meal was cooking Tom got a beer out of the refrigerator and went into the living room to watch the news, only to be interrupted by his kids asking him to play horse for them.

Tom got down on all fours. "Climb on board."

Anna and Jeremy climbed on their dad's back. "Giddy up!"

Tom started to crawl around on the floor, rearing up a little but being careful to not knock them off.

After a little time went by, Karen called, "Dinner's ready."

Anna and Jeremy climbed off their dad.

Tom said, "Go wash your hands."

They ran to the bathroom to wash their hands and fought over the faucet. Tom could hear them arguing over it.

Tom called out to them, "You had better not be fighting in there."

Both called back in unison, "We're not."

Tom walked out into the kitchen and washed his hands in the sink. The kids came running out to the dining room and sat at their chairs at the table.

"Karen, is there anything that I can carry to the table?"

"Why don't you take over the chicken?"

Tom grabbed the chicken and Karen grabbed the green beans and went back for the potatoes. They all sat down to dinner. As they were eating, they started to talk more about their days.

Tom asked, "Anna, what else happened at school today?"

"I made a new friend. Her name is Julie. She is in the third grade and she stopped some boys from picking on me."

"You know those boys only pick on you because they like you."

"I don't think so. They pick on everyone that is smaller than them."

"I guess they are just bullies, then. All that you have to do with bullies is stand up to them. They don't know what to do when someone isn't afraid of them."

"What if they hurt me?"

"Then tell a teacher and don't be afraid to stand up to them again. They have to know that you will not stand for it."

"Okay, Daddy, I will."

Tom asked, "Jeremy, what happened during your day?"

"I got to finger paint today."

Karen asked, "What picture did you paint?"

"I painted a picture of a lake with a shady tree."

"Did you bring it home so that we can see it?"

"No, I had to turn it in."

"Oh, okay."

Tom said, "This dinner is really good."

"Thank you."

Anna said, "Yeah, Mommy, this is really good."

"Yes, Mommy, thank you."

"You're welcome, honey bear. You're welcome too, buddy."

As they finished up dinner, Karen said, "Now go upstairs and change into your pajamas."

The kids said in unison, "Okay, Mommy."

Anna and Jeremy ran up the stairs and into their bedrooms to change.

Tom said, "Here, let me help you with the dishes."

"I will take you up on that."

Tom stood up and started to clear the table as Karen started to put the leftovers away. Tom started the dishes when he got the table cleared.

"Wow, there are a lot of dishes with this meal."

"Yeah, I tried to keep up with them, but I just gave up."

"That's okay, I like a challenge. I did marry you."

"Very funny, good because you have a challenge," Karen said. "I'm going to go check on the kids."

"Okay, I will finish up here."

"Thank you."

"You're welcome."

Karen left and went to check on the kids, who were playing in their rooms.

"It's time to go to bed! Brush your teeth!"

The kids ran out of their rooms and into the bathroom to brush their teeth.

While Jeremy ran by, he said, "She isn't kidding. She will check."

"That is right."

When the kids came out of the bathroom, Karen followed Jeremy into his room.

"Goodnight, buddy."

"Goodnight, Mommy."

Karen then walked over to Anna's room and walked in to find Anna playing on her floor.

"Come on now, get into bed."

"Okay, Mommy. I'm sorry."

"It's okay, it's just time to go to sleep. Goodnight, honey bear."

"Goodnight, Mommy."

Karen walked back downstairs to find Tom just finishing up the dishes and cleaning the kitchen.

"How are the kids? Are they in bed?"

"Yes, reluctantly, but they went. What do you want to do now?"

"I just want to watch some mindless television."

Tom and Karen settled down and cuddled up together on the couch to watch some TV. After about two hours they turned it off.

Tom said, "It's been a long day. I think I'm going to go to bed."

"I'm going to come up with you. I'm tired as well."

Tom and Karen started up the stairs.

Karen said, "I want to check on the kids first."

Karen and Tom looked in on Anna first; she was asleep on her side under her blankets. Then they walked over to Jeremy's bedroom. They opened his door and looked in on him. He was lying on his stomach with his head turned to the side facing the door and a little drool was falling out of his mouth.

Karen turned to Tom. "Aren't they cute?"

"Yes, they are. Come on, let's go to bed."

Tom and Karen went into their bedroom and got ready for bed. They lay down in bed and started kissing.

Tom said, "Really?"

"Aren't you in the mood?"

"I could be persuaded."

They kissed some more.

THURSDAY

The sun came up and Tom woke up early. He found himself to be in a great mood. He walked downstairs, waking up his kids on the way.

"Anna, Jeremy, time to get up for school. Get ready and come down for breakfast."

Tom got downstairs and decided to make pancakes for breakfast. He figured that he would try to make Karen's life easier by making breakfast for everyone. The kids came down and sat at the table, patiently waiting for breakfast.

"Are you both ready for a pancake breakfast?"

They both said in unison, "Yes!"

Tom started to put plates on the table for Anna and Jeremy. Karen walked out from the staircase to find her family just starting to enjoy a breakfast that she didn't have to cook.

"Well, this is a nice surprise."

"I thought that breakfast would be nice to wake up to for you."

Karen responded by walking over and giving Tom a passionate kiss.

The kids both said, "Eww!"

Then she said, "Thank you for last night. It was great."

"I enjoyed it as well."

"What happened last night?" Anna asked. "Sounds like it was fun."

Tom and Karen said in unison, "Never mind!"

Karen said, "We will tell you when you're older."

As the family ate breakfast, they enjoyed each other's company.

"What do you kids have going on at school today?"

"We have a spelling test tomorrow," stated Anna. "So, I think we are going over the words today."

"We are working on the calendar today."

"Sounds like a full day," Tom said. "Well, I'm going to head in early, so I will see everyone later. I love all of you."

Tom kissed Karen goodbye and waved to his children, then walked out the door. He got into his car and drove down the street, seeing kids walking to the bus stop.

Tom walked into the office to find Mike already there.

"I'm going to run John Murphy through the system to see if he has a record," declared Tom.

Tom went to the computer to run his name through the system.

"Did anything come up?"

"His name popped. He has several arrests for possession. He did two years for it and got out a year ago."

"Well, if he has done it once than he might have done it again. That might be why Kathy broke up with him. He might have needed to shut her up for something that she saw or heard."

"That would be a good motive! We need to go talk to him."

"Did his file say where he was working?"

Tom declared, "Yes it says that he works at the 7-11 down on 7th Street."

Mike and Tom walked out and drove down to the 7th Street 7-11.

"Maybe I should drive."

"I'm good to drive," Mike responded. "There isn't any rain today."

"You are a good driver. You just don't react to other drivers so well."

"I just get annoyed when I'm in traffic."

"I think everyone does. It's just how you react to it."

"I know I need to get it under control."

When they walked through the door, John Murphy was working behind the counter. He stood about five foot eleven and had brown hair. He was wearing blue jeans and a red 7–11 polo shirt. The store was your typical convenience store, it had aisles of food on shelves. The counter was on the left side as you walked through the door. There were cigarettes on a rack behind the person working the register. There was a lottery machine on the counter with lottery tickets under the counter.

"John Murphy? I'm Detective James, and this is Detective Turner. Can we ask you a few questions?"

"Yeah sure, what about?"

"No, we would like you to come with us down to the station."

"Okay. Let me clear it with my boss. Hey, Will, these cops want me to go with them."

"Go, we will cover you."

They all walked out together and got into the car.

"Can't you tell me what this is all about?"

"We will soon enough," Tom told him.

When they got there, they directed him into an interrogation room. It was small, just a small table with three chairs around it. There was a mirror in one wall; otherwise, the room was empty. As they walked into the room John acted like he was the only one that mattered. He was cocky and acted like he didn't have a care in the world.

Mike said, "Have a seat. We want to know about your relationship with Kathy Jefferson."

"Why, what did she say about me?"

"She didn't say anything. When was the last time that you saw her?"

"It was about a week and a half ago. I was at her house talking to her about our relationship and our future."

"Is that what you call it?" asked Tom. "We heard that she broke up with you and you weren't taking it so well."

"We were taking a break and I was trying to convince her to come back to me. What's going on? Is she saying that I'm harassing her or something?"

"She was found dead yesterday morning. Where were you on Sunday between the hours of 1 and 5 pm?"

John's attitude changed when he found out that Kathy was dead. He became nervous and upset, even a little angry.

"I thought that she was found yesterday?"

Mike said, "She was but she was killed on Sunday afternoon."

"I was at work from about 1:50 to 10 that evening. Before that I was getting ready for work at home. You can check it."

"Don't worry," Tom said. "We will."

"If you want to know who could have done something to her you should look into someone at school. She left me for someone, but I don't know who. She was secretive about who it was."

Mike asked, "Why do you say that?"

"Well, I wanted to know who it was so that I could tell them to back off, but she would never tell me who it was, and I never saw anyone new come by her house."

Tom responded, "You were watching her?"

"Well, I would drive by her house every once in a while, so I wouldn't say that I was watching her, just checking in."

"Well, we will be checking in on you so don't go too far. You can go for now."

John walked out of the room and Tom closed the door as they went to their desks. Their desks were at the back of the room facing each other. They grabbed their jackets as they left their desks and headed for the door.

"I guess we should head back to the store to check his alibi."

Mike responded, "Okay, but we need to stop to get something to eat first."

"Do you ever get enough to eat? It seems that you always want to eat."

"Can I help it if I'm always hungry?"

"I guess not. Come on, let's get you something to eat."

"Sounds good to me!"

"I'm sure that it does."

Tom and Mike proceeded to their car. Tom got in the passenger's side and Mike got into the driver's side. They exited out of the driveway headed to lunch.

Tom stated, "Okay, I want some good old-fashioned American food. Let's go to the local diner for lunch."

"Which diner are you thinking?"

"I was thinking Mel's Diner."

"That actually sounds good. Let's go."

They drove up to the diner where there was a small parking lot that wrapped around the back of the restaurant. They parked at the back of the parking lot and started to walk in.

"Why do you always park at the back of the lot?" asked Tom.

"Because we can walk the distance, there are some people that can't. I park at the back of the lot so that I'm doing my part to help those that can't."

"That makes sense. Okay, you're off the hook."

Tom and Mike walked into the restaurant and immediately smelled the scent of grilled burgers and fries. The air felt like oil. There were brown vinyl booths lining the walls and free-standing metal tables with wooden tops in the middle of the room and metal chairs with brown vinyl seats. There was a breakfast bar at the back of the room with stationary stools surrounding it with metal back and brown vinyl seats. The restaurant was about half full of regular customers sitting at the bar and in various booths and tables around the room.

Tom said, "This is a real American diner."

"Yeah. I can feel the grease on me now."

"Let's find a table."

They sat down at a table in the front corner of the restaurant. There was a tear in the vinyl seat on the right side where Tom sat. A few minutes later the waitress, who was wearing a rose-colored uniform shirt and blue jeans with a name tag on it that read Ashley, walked over.

"Can I get you something to drink to start?"

Tom said, "I will have an iced tea."

"I will have a Coke."

"I will be back in a few minutes to take your order, unless you're ready now?"

Tom replied, "I'm ready now."

"Me too."

"What will it be?"

Mike said, "I'll have the double cheeseburger and fries."

"And you?"

"What kind of cheese do you have for the cheeseburger?"

"It's American cheese, I think."

"Oh, could you substitute cheddar cheese instead? I'm lactose intolerant."

"I can look into it. If not cheddar cheese, then?"

"That's right. I want the double cheeseburger, but I want onion rings instead of fries."

"Okay, got it."

Then she walked away.

"You can eat cheddar cheese when you're lactose intolerant?"

"Yes, there are a few cheeses that you can have because the lactose is so minimal that it won't bother you if you're lactose intolerant. Karen found out for me. I have been enjoying cheese again. It's been great."

A couple of minutes later the food came and filled the air with the greasy food that they just ordered.

Tom said, "This is perfect."

They both grabbed their burgers and took a bite.

"This is so good."

Mike concurred, "This really hits the spot."

They finished their lunch eating instead of talking and when they got done, they waited for the bill.

"That was good. I hope that we are able to catch some of the victim's friends before they go home for the day because it will make it a lot harder to track them down."

"Yeah, I agree. Well, maybe we can catch one of her classes before they go."

Ashley brought the check and said, "Just pay up front when you're ready."

Tom looked at Mike and asked, "Are you ready?"

"Yeah I'm ready."

Tom and Mike got up, left $8 for a tip, and walked to the front counter and waited to pay.

The cashier walked up and asked, "Did you enjoy everything?"

Tom said, "We did, thank you."

"Your total is $16.07."

Tom handed him a 20.

"Your change is $3.93."

"Thank you."

Tom and Mike walked out of the restaurant and to the car. They got in and put on their seatbelts.

Mike said, "Now, let's stop by the 7–11 and check Murphy's alibi."

"That was my plan."

"What do you think about this guy?"

"I like this guy for it. But if his alibi holds, I don't know where to go next."

"Being at work is the definition of a rock-solid alibi, isn't it?"

"Yeah, but there has got to be hole in it somewhere."

When they pulled into the driveway, the parking lot was full, so they had to park on the side of the building. Tom and Mike walked in and went directly to see the manager. They walked up to the employee behind the counter, who was about five foot eleven inches tall with brown hair wearing a red polo shirt and blue jeans with brown hiking boots and a name tag that said Rick.

Tom said, "We need to speak to your manager."

"Okay, I will go get him."

Rick disappeared into the back of the store and then a few minutes later the manager walked out.

The manager said, "Hi, I'm Will, the manager. How can I help you?"

"Hello, I'm Detective Turner and this is Detective James. We need to verify that John Murphy was working here on Sunday between the hours of 1:50 and 10 pm."

"Well according to his time card, he was here during those times. Here is something interesting, though."

Tom said, "What's that?"

"According to this, he clocked in at 1:57 pm for his shift and then clocked out again for an early lunch at about 3:03 pm and clocked back in at 4:36pm."

"Do your employees usually clock out for lunch right after they clock in?"

"No, they don't even usually clock out for lunch because they take a paid lunch. Rick was working with him so let me ask him."

Will yelled, "Hey, Rick, come over here."

Rick walked over from the soda machine.

"What is it, boss?"

"Why did John clock out an hour after clocking in on Sunday?"

"Oh, he said that he had an errand to run and I told him that it was fine with me, I would watch the store, but he had to clock out for it so that I don't get in trouble for covering it up if he got caught."

Tom asked, "Do you know what the errand was?"

"I don't have any idea. I'm sorry that I couldn't be more help."

"Don't worry, you were a big help," Mike said. "Oh, it would be a good idea for you to not tell him that you told us about Sunday. Thank you both for your time."

Tom and Mike started to walk out of the store.

Tom turned to Mike and said, "It looks like another alibi that is shaky."

"I think that we need to talk to John Murphy again. But it's getting late, so I guess we can go see him in the morning."

"True, so I will see you in the morning."

"Sounds good. Have a good night."

"Good night."

Tom walked out and got into his car to drive home when he got a call from Karen.

"Hi, honey. Would you do me a favor?"

"Yes, what is it?"

"Would you please stop by the store and pick up a few things for me?"

"What do you need?"

"We need a gallon of milk, a dozen and a half eggs, 2 loaves of bread, and Elmer's Glue."

"I get the other stuff but why do we need glue?"

"We need the glue for a class project. Your daughter is learning the planets and has to put together a solar system for next week."

"Sounds like fun. Okay, I'll stop and then I will be home."

Tom drove to the store and pulled into the parking lot. He was in luck; there was a spot right up front. A car was leaving right when he pulled in. He parked and walked in. The store was packed with early evening shoppers. There was an assortment of characters walking through the store. Some were people sent to the store after work like Tom was. Others were stay-at-home parents that forgot to go during the day, they were dragging their bored kids through the store. Some were working people that didn't get have other time to go to the store. They decided not to go on the weekend because no matter how crowded it is in the evening it is worse on the weekend. The store had aisles going from the front to the back of the store. The dairy was situated in the back of the store and the less common things were in the front of the store. Tom grabbed a shopping cart and walked the store, finding the milk first at the back along with the eggs. Tom then walked to the left side of the store to find the bread aisle to get some bread. Then he had to find the school supply aisle.

Tom found an employee and asked, "Could you tell me where the Elmer's Glue is?"

"Yes, I can. It is the second to the last aisle, aisle 23."

"Thank you."

"You're welcome."

Tom walked away and toward the school supply aisle on the other side of the store. Once he got to the aisle, he walked halfway down to find the glue. Then he turned and walked to the checkout line. When he got to the checkout, he was third in line. He felt like he was getting lucky all the way around. First, he got a parking spot in front and then only third in line at the checkout. He waited patiently for his turn.

When he got to the front the cashier said, "Hello, how are you doing tonight?"

"Hi, I'm doing good. How about you?"

"We are busy, so time is flying by so it's good. Did you find everything that you needed tonight?"

"Yes, I did eventually."

"That will be $11.95."

Tom handed the cashier $20.

"Here is your change, 12, 13, 14, 15, and 20."

"Thank you. Have a good night."

"You too. Good night."

Tom walked out of the store and back to the car. He pulled out and almost backed into another car as they were driving through the parking lot. He finally got out of his spot and drove out of the parking lot. He was finally headed home after a long day at work. Tom reached his house and gathered up the groceries and went into the house.

As Tom walked into the house he hollered, "Is anyone here?"

Karen yelled back, "We are upstairs. We will be down in a minute."

Tom walked into the kitchen to put the groceries away. He saw some textbooks on one side of the table and some folded clothes on the other. Karen came into the room and gave Tom a kiss hello.

"Sorry, we were upstairs putting away laundry. How was your day?"

"It was okay. What's for dinner?"

"Well, it was a busy day, so I thought that we could just order a pizza tonight. What do you think?"

"I guess I don't have much of a choice if there isn't anything made."

"I'm sorry."

"Don't worry about it, I was just kidding. Pizza sounds good for tonight."

"Ha ha very funny."

"I figured that you had it coming after sending me to the store on a Thursday night after work. It was very busy."

"What kind do you want?"

"How about the usual? A supreme for us and a pepperoni for the kids."

"You know with two pizzas there will be leftovers."

"That is the point. You know how I like pizza leftovers."

"True."

"Where are the kids?"

"They are upstairs. Jeremy is in the tub and Anna is playing in her room waiting her turn."

"Why don't you go have the kids switch and I will order the pizza."

Karen walked up the stairs and Tom picked up the phone to call in their order.

"Jeremy, it's time to get out of the tub. Rinse off, dry off, and put on your pajamas. Anna, get your stuff together so that you can get in the tub."

Karen got to the top of the stairs as Jeremy was coming out of the bathroom.

"I'm all done, Mommy. Can I go downstairs and see Daddy?"

"Yes, you can, buddy. Come on, Anna, it's your turn."

Anna came out of her bedroom and ran into the bathroom for her bath.

"Don't run, honey bear."

"Sorry, Mommy."

The bathroom door shut with her apology. Karen walked back down the stairs to find Tom drinking a beer and relaxing in his chair with Jeremy sitting with him.

"Did you order the pizza?"

"Yes, I did."

"Then why don't you help me clear the table of the rest of this laundry and Anna's books so that we can eat when it gets here?"

"Okay, I'm coming. I will be out there in a minute."

Tom took a drink of his beer and got up and headed to the kitchen.

"Why don't you take the rest of the kids' clothes up to their rooms and put them away? I will take care of Anna's books and set the table."

"Okay, if you insist."

Tom walked upstairs with the clothes. He walked into Jeremy's room first and put his shirts in his top dresser drawer. Then he walked into Anna's room and put her shirts in her second drawer down. As he was coming out of Anna's room Anna came out of the bathroom from her bath.

"Daddy!"

"Hi, princess. Hurry up; dinner will be here soon."

"What is for dinner?"

"Pizza."

"Yay! I'm coming right now."

Tom and Anna headed back downstairs just as the doorbell rang.

"I will get it."

Tom walked over to the door with Anna at his feet. He opened the door and there was a young man standing there wearing a blue polo shirt with the restaurant logo on it with blue jeans and brown tennis shoes holding a red warming envelope.

"Did you order a couple of pizzas? A supreme and a pepperoni?"

"That would be us."

"That will be $24.93."

Tom handed him $30 and said, "Keep the change."

"Thank you, enjoy your pizza. Have a good night."

"You too and drive safely."

Tom walked in with Anna to the kitchen with the pizza.

"Dinner is served. I worked hard on it."

"You dialed the phone."

"Well, the phone was heavy."

"All right. Let's sit down and eat."

Everyone sat down at their place at the table. They put their napkins on their laps and opened the boxes.

Tom asked, "Jeremy, do you want pepperoni?"

"Yeah."

"Anna, do you also want pepperoni?"

"Yes please."

Tom reached for the peperoni and put a slice on each of his kids' plates. Then he moved the pepperoni pizza under the supreme pizza and took a slice. Then Karen took a slice.

"This is a well-rounded meal. Get it, it's a circle?"

"Yes, I get it," Karen responded. "You tell that joke every time that we have pizza for dinner."

Tom asked, "Anna, what is going on with you at school? Don't you have a spelling test tomorrow?"

"Yes, I'm nervous about it."

"Well, didn't you study?"

"I did, I just don't like tests."

Karen said, "Most of us don't but it's how you handle it that matters."

"What's going on at school for you Jeremy?" asked Tom.

"We have been working on the calendar and I keep forgetting a month."

"Which month?"

"I don't know."

Karen said, "Why don't you name the months that you know?"

"Okay." Holding up his fingers, he counted off, "January, February, March, April, June, July, August, September, October, November, December. See? I always forget one."

"The one you're forgetting is an easy one to forget," Tom said. "It's May."

"Oh yeah, May. How can I remember that one?"

Karen said, "Just try to remember that there are two that start with the letter M."

"Okay, I'll try."

Tom asked Karen, "So what was your day like today?"

"You know, cleaning, laundry, getting the kids to and from the bus stop. All fun and games."

"You know every time that I don't want to go to work and I'm thinking about staying home all I have to do is ask you about your day and the feeling goes away."

"Gee, thanks, dear."

"I love you."

"I love you too."

Tom said, "Okay, kids, put your plates in the sink and go play until bedtime."

The kids got up and went to put their plates in the sink, but Jeremy couldn't reach the sink.

"Anna, please help your brother."

"Okay, Mommy."

Anna reached down and took Jeremy's plate from him and put it into the sink. Then they ran off to play in their rooms.

Tom said, "Here let me help you with the dishes."

"Hey, you're helping without me asking you to or telling you to."

"I help."

Karen said under her breath, "When I don't give you choice."

"What was that?"

"I didn't say anything."

"I heard you say something."

"I said I love you." She smiled.

"Yeah right. I love you too."

"What do you want to do tonight?"

"I just want to relax."

"How about we put the kids to bed, make some popcorn and watch a movie?"

"That sounds perfect. I would love to curl up with you."

"Okay. Why don't we go and check on the kids together tonight? I'm sure that they would love that."

"Sounds good."

Tom and Karen walked up the stairs together to check on the kids. They came to Anna's room first. They walked in and saw Anna playing with her dolls on the floor.

Karen said, "Anna, it's time for bed."

"But, Mommy, I want to stay up longer."

"How about this?" Tom asked. "We will go put your brother to bed first and then we will be back but there will be no complaints. Okay?"

"Okay."

"Come on, sweetie, let's go put Jeremy down first."

As they walked out, Karen turned to Tom and said, "You're too soft on her."

"Yeah maybe, but she is my little princess."

"Yeah. Just be careful with it."

"I am being careful. I watch what I let her get away with. Besides, she is older. We should think about letting her stay up later."

"Okay, we can talk about it, later."

They then walked into Jeremy's room to find him playing with his cars.

"Come on, Jeremy, it's time for you to go to bed."

"Okay, Daddy."

Jeremy climbed into bed and said, "I'm ready."

Karen bent down and gave him a kiss goodnight. Then Tom bent down and gave him a kiss goodnight.

"Sleep tight, buddy. I love you."

"Good night, champ. I love you."

"Good night, Mommy and Daddy. I love you too."

Karen and Tom walked out of Jeremy's room and turned off the light. Then they walked back into Anna's room.

Karen said, "Okay, Anna, now it's time for bed."

"Okay, Mommy."

Tom said, "I told you no complaining."

"Okay, Daddy."

Anna climbed up into bed. Karen bent down and gave her a kiss good night. Then Tom bent down and kissed her good night.

"Good night, princess. I love you."

"Good night, honey bear. I love you."

"Good night, Mommy and Daddy. I love you too."

Tom and Karen walked back down the stairs together.

Karen turned to Tom and asked, "What movie do you want to watch?"

"Well, it's your turn to pick."

"Okay, then I want to watch one of the Hallmark movies that we have recorded."

"Oh, goody. A chick flick."

"I gave you an option and you said that it was my turn."

"I know. It's okay. I won't complain."

Karen went into the kitchen and started to make some popcorn.

"How much butter do you want on it, honey?"

"You know me. I like a lot, turn it yellow."

"Okay."

Karen brought in the popcorn and Tom had gotten out a blanket for them to share. They sat down on the couch and curled up together. They picked out a Hallmark movie and leaned back to watch. Halfway through the movie Karen looked up at her husband and saw that he had fallen asleep. She thought to herself, Forget him. I'm going to finish my movie. After the movie was over, she woke up Tom.

"Honey, come on, wake up. Let's go to bed."

"I went to sleep?"

"Yes, you did. You fell asleep halfway through."

"I'm sorry, sweetie. I didn't mean to."

"I know but I think that it's time for bed."

"Yeah, I agree."

Tom took the popcorn bowl out to the kitchen and they headed up to bed. When they got to their bedroom, they started to change clothes.

"How's your case going?"

"It's running me in circles so far, but we will get it figured out."

"I'm sure that you will. I have faith in you."

"I'm really tired."

"Yeah me too. A good night's sleep is what I really need."

"I know what you mean."

They lay down in bed, cuddled up together, and fell asleep in each other's arms.

FRIDAY

The next morning, they woke up together when their alarms went off.

Karen asked, "Do you want to take a shower with me to save on water?"

"You know how I like to save money."

"I know I'm using that knowledge to take advantage of you."

"I would love to take a shower with you."

They went into the shower.

Karen and Tom got dressed and walked downstairs to find Anna and Jeremy watching cartoons on TV.

Karen said, "Come on, kids. You have to get ready for school."

"Okay, Mommy," Anna said. "We are."

The kids went running up the stairs to get dressed and ready for school. Karen went into the kitchen to start breakfast. She went to the refrigerator and got out the eggs and bacon. She got out a frying pan and started to fry the bacon.

Tom came into the room and asked, "What's for breakfast?"

"I figured that if I didn't use the eggs that I made you get I would be in trouble."

"You are right. You would be in a lot of trouble, like no more showers like this morning."

"You're all bark and no bite."

"I could change."

"I won't hold my breath."

Tom walked up behind her and kissed her on the cheek.

"See, you can't resist me."

"Yeah I know, I'm helpless."

Karen yelled, "Kids, come on, breakfast is ready."

The kids came running around the corner to their chairs.

"Stop running in the house!"

Anna said, "Sorry, Mommy."

Karen looked at Tom. "Can you help me with this stuff?"

Tom walked over and grabbed the kids' plates and Karen grabbed their plates. They set all the plates on the table and they all sat down to breakfast.

Tom asked, "Anna, are you ready for your spelling test today?"

"I hope so. I studied, but I'm not good at spelling."

"You will do fine. Just remember I'm proud of you no matter what."

"Thank you, Daddy. I love you."

Karen asked, "Jeremy, how are you doing with your months?"

"I keep reminding myself that there are two months that start with the letter M."

"That's good, Jeremy. You will do fine."

"Thank you, Mommy."

Tom asked Karen, "What do you have planned for today?"

"I planned on taking the kids to school, I have some errands to run, and then I'm going to have lunch with the girls."

"I hope that you have fun with that. I need to get going. I have to interrogate someone this morning."

Anna said, "That is so cool."

"Everyone have a great day! I love you all!"

Tom walked over and gave Karen a kiss goodbye and walked out of the house. He got in his car and drove to work. When he got to the office, Mike was already there.

Mike said, "I looked up John Murphy's address. So, are we ready to go?"

"Let me get a cup of coffee and then we can go."

"Why don't we just stop and get a good cup of coffee on the way?"

"Okay, you twisted my arm, but let me make a call first."

"Who are you going to call?"

"I'm going to call the medical examiner to find out about the autopsy report."

"That's a good idea. That report would be helpful in finding out who killed her."

Tom dialed the number to the medical examiner's office.

"Hello?"

Tom said, "Hello, this is Detective James. I was calling about autopsy for Kathy Jefferson?"

"Hi, Detective. This is Doctor Johnson. The autopsy report is almost ready. We should be ready for you to come down on Monday."

"Thank you, we will see you on Monday then. Goodbye."

"Bye."

Tom and Mike walked out of the station to their car. They drove to the nearest Starbucks. The store was small, with an outside terrace with open umbrellas at each table and four chairs sitting by the table. The inside had a counter with a glass display case filled with pastries. There were five tables with four chairs at each table. There was a barista at the order counter wearing a green polo shirt with khaki pants.

"What can I get you?"

Mike stepped forward. "I would like a chai tea and whatever he wants. It's on me."

"What size would you like?"

"Venti."

"Your name?"

"Mike."

"And can I get something for you?"

"Thank you, I would like a mocha latte."

The barista asked, "Name? What size would you like?"

Tom said, "Tom. Venti."

"That will be $10.14."

"Here is $12. Keep the change."

"Thank you. They will be right out."

"Thank you."

After an unusually long wait, Tom asked, "What is taking so long? We have things to do."

"Mike, Mike."

"Right here. Thank you."

"Tom, Tom."

"Over here. Thank you."

Tom and Mike left the Starbucks and headed over to John Murphy's house.

Tom said, "This address looks like it's in a bad area of town."

"It is the bad part of town. I don't even feel safe going there with you."

"That's bad, because you never seem to be afraid of anything."

"It will be okay. It can just be a dangerous place to be, especially if you're a cop."

As they started to drive into the neighborhood, the houses looked rundown. John Murphy's house was single story and had a chain link around the front yard with a Pitbull running back and forth kicking up the dirt in the front yard. The roof needed repair. The shingles looked loose and were rippled and breaking. The house was white with light blue trim. It had a window in front with light blue shutters. There was a single dead tree in the front dirt yard. There was a single-car detached garage to the right of the house. As they walked up to the house the dog was going crazy.

Tom yelled, "Hey, John Murphy!"

John walked out. "What?"

"You need to control your dog."

"Come here, Max!"

The dog turned and ran into the house. John shut the door behind it.

"You need to come with us to the station."

"Do you have a warrant?"

"Do you really want to go that far?"

"Okay, okay. I will go with you."

John followed Mike back to their car with Tom following close behind him. Tom sat in the back seat with John. They drove back to the station in complete silence. When they got back to the station, they escorted John into the back door of the station and guided him back to the interrogation room. John sat in the room alone for some time. They observed him walking around the room nervously. He couldn't seem to sit still.

Tom said, "You can tell a lot about a suspect when you leave them alone in the room for a while. Their behavior will show whether they are calm or nervous."

"Do you think that it is time to go in and see where he was when he said that he was at work?"

"Yeah, I guess he has been stewing enough. Let's go see what he has to say."

Tom and Mike walked into the room and shut the door.

Mike said, "Sit down!"

John walked over and sat at the table opposite Tom and Mike.

"What is this about?" He nervously tapped his foot.

Tom said, "Well, your alibi fell apart."

"You said that you were at work during our time of death window."

"Yes, that is right."

Tom said, "You left something out, didn't you?"

"What do you mean?"

Mike declared, "You left out that you left work for an hour and a half during our time of death window."

"Oh, I forgot about that."

Tom said, "You forgot about it? This doesn't look good for you John!"

"I just wasn't thinking."

"You weren't thinking?"

"Where were you during the time between 3 and 4:30 pm?" Mike asked.

"I went to the pharmacy."

Tom asked, "You went to the pharmacy, why?"

"My mom is sick and that morning I took her to the doctor before work. On my way to work I dropped off her prescription and I needed to get it to her."

"Which pharmacy did you go to?"

"I went to Walgreens."

"Which one?"

"It's the one on 1st and Main."

Mike asked, "What was the prescription for?"

"It was antibiotics. She has a sinus infection."

"Is there anything else that you would like to add?"

"No, that's where I was. I went to the pharmacy and then I went home to take the medication to my mom so that she could get started on them right away."

Tom said, "Okay then, you can go, but you better believe that we will be checking your alibi."

"Okay, thank you."

John left the room. Tom turned to Mike. "I just don't see how it would take an hour and a half to pick up medications and take them home."

"Maybe there was a line at the pharmacy."

"Yeah maybe. I guess we will find out when we go and ask."

Tom and Mike walked out of the interrogation room for Tom to find his phone on his desk ringing.

"Hello?"

"Hello, this is Sergeant Gonzales at the front desk. I have a Mr. and Mrs. Jefferson here. They were wondering if you could talk with them about their daughter's case."

"Sure, I will be right up to get them. Thank you, Sergeant."

Tom hung up the phone and turned to Mike. "The Jeffersons are up front I'm going to go get them so that we can update them on the case."

"I hate when they want updates. I never know what to tell them."

Tom walked through the maze of desks and chairs to the front to greet the Jeffersons.

"Hello, Mr. Jefferson, Mrs. Jefferson." He shook their hands.

"Please call me Paul."

"Please call me Susan."

"Well, Paul, Susan, if you will follow me this way, we will find someplace private to talk."

Tom escorted them through the door and then through the maze of desks and chairs to a private room where, Mike was waiting for them.

Mike stood up. "Hello again, Mr. Jefferson, Mrs. Jefferson." He shook their hands.

"They would like to be called Paul and Susan."

Paul asked, "So where are we with the case?"

Tom responded, "We are still questioning friends of Kathy's."

"What about her ex-boyfriend? Have you talked to him?"

"Yes. We talked to him a couple of times, but he has an alibi."

Susan asked, "Well, are you just taking his word for it? Because he isn't trustworthy."

"Don't worry. We are checking everyone's alibi."

"Okay, good."

"They should be done with the autopsy early next week so then we will know more about how she died," Mike said. "At that time, you should be able to come in and identify her body and we will go over the parts of the report with you that we can."

Paul asked, "You can't go over all of it?"

Tom stated, "Well, there might be information pertinent to the investigation."

"Okay, well, thank you for your time and tolerating our interruption. I think that it's time that we got out of your way."

"It's no problem at all. Any time that you have questions you are more than welcome to contact us. We are here to help."

Paul and Susan stood up and shook Tom's and Mike's hands.

"Have a better day. We will be in contact. Can you find your way out?"

Paul replied, "Yes we will find it, thank you again."

Paul and Susan walked out.

Mike said, "That just breaks my heart."

"Well, let's get some lunch, then we will head over to check on that alibi."

"That's different."

"What is that?"

"You were the one to suggest lunch."

"Well, I'm hungry."

"Let's go then."

"I didn't think that you would argue with me."

They grabbed their jackets and walked out the door, headed to the car.

Mike asked, "Where do you want to go for lunch?"

"I was thinking about going back to Mel's Diner. I want another one of their burgers."

"Okay, I guess I can give you this one. But I get to choose next time."

"Okay, that works for me."

"What are your plans for the weekend?"

"I have a wonderful day planned tomorrow for the kids."

"What are you going to do?"

"I heard about this ranch that has working Hangin' Tree Cattle Dogs that just had puppies about eight weeks ago and they are ready to go," Tom said. "So, I'm taking the kids out to get one."

"What is a Hangin' Tree Cattle Dog?"

"I don't know but I do know that it is a newer breed and they are really rare."

"They are really going to love you for this."

"I know. I just have to get Karen to sign off on it tonight."

"You haven't gotten her okay yet? Good luck."

"Thanks. I'm going to need it."

They pulled into the driveway and parked all the way in the back of the parking lot again.

Tom said with frustration, "I wish just one time I could have a short walk to the door."

"Become handicapped."

They walked into the restaurant and it was a little more crowded than it was before. The dining area was full and there was one table available. The rest of the restaurant was filled with the lunch rush.

Tom said, "It's really crowded in here."

"Do you want to go somewhere else?"

"No, I still want one of their cheeseburgers. Let's grab that last table."

"Okay then, we will stay."

They walked over and sat down at the last table. Then a familiar face walked over. It was the same waitress that they had the day before.

"Hey, you're back! Would you like some menus?"

Tom said, "I don't need one."

"You sound like someone that knows what you want. What about you?"

"I'm good, I know what I want too."

"Then what will it be?"

"I will have one of those cheeseburgers with cheddar cheese and onion rings."

"What do you want to drink?"

"Oh yeah, I will have iced tea."

"What about you?"

"I also want a cheeseburger but with fries and I want a Coke to drink."

"Okay. I will get this order in for you."

"So how are you going to approach your wife about this dog idea?"

"I was thinking that I would appeal to her childhood."

"Here are your drinks, enjoy."

"What do you mean?"

"Well, she grew up with dogs and she wanted a dog when we first got together but we lived in an apartment and didn't have room for one."

"That's one way to do it."

"Hey, our food is here."

The waitress came walking up with a tray full of food.

"Okay, here we go. A cheeseburger with cheddar cheese and onion rings here and a cheeseburger with fries here. Is there anything else that you guys need?"

Tom replied, "No, I think that we are good. Thank you."

"Okay. Enjoy, guys."

"I've been looking forward to this all morning."

"So, you had this planned out before talking to me, huh?"

"What can I say? I had a craving."

"Can I get one of your onion rings?"

"Sure, I guess," Tom said. "Why don't you ever get your own?"

"Because I never want a full order and you always get them, so I figure I can just steal one of yours."

"One of these times I'm going to say no just to mess with you."

"Very funny. Could you pass the ketchup?"

"Here you go."

The waitress came back to see how things were going.

"How are we doing?"

Tom said, "I don't know about him, but I think that I want a piece of pie."

"What kind would you like?"

"I think that I want apple pie."

"Okay, and do you want some pie?"

"Yes, I think that I will have a piece of peach pie with a scoop of ice cream."

"Okay. I will bring those right out."

As they finished their burgers, the waitress came back with their pies.

"Here you go, guys. Enjoy."

Tom was digging into his pie as he said, "This is perfect."

"I would have to agree. It's nice to have something for me when we are working on a case like this one."

The waitress walked over and put the check on the table. Mike picked it up and looked at it. It said that the total was $24.97.

"Just pay up front when you are ready."

Mike asked, "Are you ready?"

"As ready as I will ever be."

Mike and Tom walked up to the front counter, leaving a $9 tip, and waited for someone to come up front to take their money.

The cashier walked up and asked, "Did you enjoy everything?"

Mike said, "Yes we did. It was really good today."

"Your total is $24.97."

"Here you go." He handed him $25.

"Thank you, your change is $0.03. Have a good day."

"Thank you. You have a good day too."

Tom and Mike walked out of the door and to the back of the parking lot. They got into the car and drove away, headed to John Murphy's house to talk to his mother.

Mike asked, "What do you think that his mother will say?"

"It depends on whether or not he gets to her first."

"Do you really think that she will cover for him?"

"It's possible. Mothers are always unpredictable when it comes to protecting their babies."

"He's not exactly a baby."

"That doesn't matter," Tom said. "To her he is still her baby who can't do any wrong."

"I never looked at it like that."

"Yeah, mothers are funny that way. I once had a suspect's mother cover for her son when there was a witness that talked to him at the scene. The worse part about it is she didn't need to cover for him because he didn't do it. Then there was another time when a mother asked to testify against her son because she was so sure that he was guilty, and he was innocent too."

"That's crazy."

"Yeah, mothers are a bit crazy. You never know how they are going to react when you challenge them to protect their young."

"Well, I guess we are about to find out how she is going to react. We are here."

Mike parked the car on the street, they walked up to the house. When they got to the gate they looked around and the dog was nowhere in sight.

Tom looked at Mike and asked, "Do you think that it is safe?"

"I don't see him. Let's give it a shot."

They lifted the latch on the gate and walked through. When they got to the door Mike knocked and they heard Max start barking. Then they heard a voice from the back of the house.

A woman yelled, "Max, shut the hell up!"

The door opened and standing there was a woman in her late fifties wearing a purple plaid shirt with blue jeans and gray tennis shoes. She stood about five foot seven inches tall with long brown hair.

"What do you want?"

"Hello, I'm Detective James, and this is Detective Turner..."

"I know who you are. Ask your questions."

Mike asked, "For our record, what is your name?"

"Sharon Murphy."

"Did you know Kathy Jefferson?"

"Yes, I knew her. I liked her until she broke my son's heart. The little tramp went off with some other guy right when she broke up with him."

"How do you know that she was dating someone else?" asked Tom.

"My son told me."

"What time did your son return home after he went to work on Tuesday?"

"He came home at 3:30 pm to bring me my medication."

"Are you sure about the time?"

"Yes, I'm sure. Now if there isn't anything else, I'm still not feeling good and I would like to go lay down for a while."

"Okay, we are done for now. We will be touch if we have more questions."

Sharon abruptly shut the door. Mike and Tom walked back to the car.

Mike asked, "Should we interview some of the neighbors to see when John really did come home to give her those medications?"

"First of all, the neighbors in this neighborhood won't talk to cops and there is no need to."

"Why is there no need?"

"Because we know that she is lying."

"How do you know she is lying?"

"Because if he got here at 3:30 then it wouldn't take another hour to get back to work."

"Okay, but how do we prove it?"

"The next stop is the pharmacy. They should have a record of the receipt of when he picked up the medication."

"Oh, I wasn't even thinking of the pharmacy."

"Let's head there next."

"Sounds good. Maybe we can get some answers."

They started to drive to the pharmacy.

Tom said, "Let's time this drive."

"Why do we want to time the drive?"

"If we know how long it takes to get to his house from the pharmacy and then how long it takes to get to his work, then we can prove that he had time to drive to the crime scene."

"That's a good idea. So, you think that John did this?"

"So far he is our strongest suspect."

"It seems that everything is pointing to him."

"Exactly. All I am doing is following the evidence."

Arriving at the pharmacy, Mike said, "Well, we are here. It took about ten minutes."

The Walgreens was situated on the corner of First and Main. It had a parking lot that wrapped around two sides of the building with the entrance positioned at the corner of the building. At the other side of the building was a drive-up window. The back of the building had a single loading dock.

Tom said, "Let's go in and find out when he was here."

Tom and Mike walked into the store and found two cash registers with an aisle in between them. The photo counter was straight back from the registers and the pharmacy was in the opposite corner from the entrance. There were aisles going from front to back and an aisle going down the middle perpendicular to all the other aisles. Mike and Tom walked to the back of the store to the pharmacy area of the store. As they walked up to the counter at the pharmacy, they saw a clerk.

"Can I help you?"

"Hello, I'm Detective James, and this is Detective Turner. Can we ask you a few questions?"

"Sure, what do you need?"

"Were you working this past Sunday?"

"I wasn't but Tasha was."

"Is Tasha working today?"

"Yes, I will get her."

The tech walked over and said, "Tasha, there are some detectives here that want to talk to you."

Tasha walked over and asked, "What can I do for you?"

"Hi, I'm Detective James, and this is Detective Turner. We need to ask you a few questions."

"What's up?"

"Were you working this past Sunday?"

"Yes, I was."

Mike asked, "Do you remember if there was a prescription picked up for a Sharon Murphy?"

"We were really busy that day, so I don't remember."

"Could you look it up?

"Let me look into it."

Tasha walked over to the pharmacist and talked to him for a few minutes. Then the pharmacist walked over.

"I'm sorry but if you want our records you will need a warrant. Because of HIPAA we can't release that information without a warrant."

"Okay, we understand. We will be back when we get that warrant."

"Good, we will be happy to help you then."

"Let's go."

Mike and Tom walked out of the store and drove away.

Tom said, "Let's drive by John's work to see how long it takes to get there."

"I believe it should be about fifteen minutes to get there. How long do you think that it will take to get a search warrant for the records at the pharmacy?"

"I'm hoping that if I get it in by tonight, we can get it back on Monday."

"That will be good, then we can verify his alibi on Monday morning."

"I still don't think that he is telling the truth. I think that his mother is covering for him."

"How are you going to approach your wife about the dog?"

"I don't know yet. I figured that I would tell her about hearing about the puppies and see what she says about that."

"So, you're hoping that she will have the idea about getting one for the kids?"

"Exactly. I figured if it's her idea then I will be off the hook."

"You're playing with fire."

"I know but it's the only way that I can see this working."

"I feel honesty is the best way to go."

"I know. I was just trying to make it easier on me."

"Well, you had better be prepared to answer questions like who is going to feed it and take care of it because you know that it's not going to be the kids. They are still too young for the responsibility."

"I know, and it will be mostly her because I will be at work. But I figure that I can help by buying a pet door so that she doesn't have to put them out all the time. At least once they got house broken."

"That's a good idea. Make it as easy as possible for her. We are here."

"How long did it take? Let's go ahead and head back to the station. I want to get that search warrant in."

"It took us about fifteen minutes, just like I said that it should."

"That means fifteen minutes to Walgreens then ten minutes to his house. With about five minutes at the store that makes Sharon Murphy's story work," Tom said. "What would it take to get from his house back here?"

"I think about fifteen minutes. Why?"

"Because unless he lied and spent more time at home than just dropping off the medication the time line doesn't add up. He should have been back at work by 3:45 to 3:50, not 4:30 pm."

"That does make sense. The time line doesn't work, does it?"

"I wonder what he did with the extra time."

"That is a good question."

"That is a question that we have to answer."

Mike and Tom pulled into the driveway of the station and started to walk in the back door.

Mike looked at Tom and said, "Why don't you go home to your family? It's getting late. I'll put in for the search warrant."

"Are you sure?"

"Yes, I'm sure. You have a long night ahead of you trying to convince Karen to go get that dog tomorrow."

"Thanks, I appreciate it."

"Good luck and good night."

"Thanks, and good night to you too."

Tom walked to his car, got in and started to drive home. He was playing the conversation in his head with his wife and he was worried that it wouldn't go his way. He wanted that dog. Tom pulled into his driveway and sat in the car for a minute to gather up his thoughts.

Tom walked in the door and hollered, "Is there anyone home?"

Karen yelled back, "We are in the kitchen!"

Tom walked into the kitchen and asked, "What's for dinner?"

"That's the first thing that you're going to say to me?"

"I'm sorry. Hi, sweetie. How was your day?"

"That's better. My day was good. How was yours?"

Anna asked, "Mommy, can we go play?"

"Yes, you can."

Tom said, "Good. I have something to talk to you about."

"What? This doesn't sound good."

"No, it's a good thing. I like to think anyways."

"You never say that we need to talk and it's a good thing besides when you start thinking I'm usually in trouble."

"Well, this one is."

"What is it?"

"You know how you wanted a dog when we first got married?"

"You want a dog."

"Not just any dog, I heard about a ranch in the country that just had Hangin' Tree Cattle Dog puppies."

"What is a Hangin' Tree Cattle Dog?"

"It is a rare dog, a newer breed."

"Who is going to feed it?" asked Karen. "Take it to the vet? Housebreak it? Clean up after it?"

"That is a lot of questions. I will do what I can and as the kids get older, they can help."

"In other words, it will be me mostly."

"Yeah, honestly, it will be."

"Well, at least you're honest about it. Let me think about it."

"Okay, but don't say anything to the kids about it just in case they don't have any left. I want to call first, and I want it to be a surprise."

"I haven't said yes yet."

"I know. I just don't want you to decide yes and blow the surprise."

"I won't," Karen said. "Now, how was your day? Did you find out anything about the ex-boyfriend?"

"Yes, the fact that he is lying, and his mother is trying to cover for him."

"Why would his mother cover for him? Doesn't she know that she could get in trouble for that?"

"I don't think that she cares."

"How do you know that he is lying?"

"Because he is missing about forty minutes in his story. We just don't know if it's at the beginning part of his story or the end."

"What's the difference?"

"If he is missing the time at the beginning part of the story then he could have committed the murder, but if it is at the end of his story then his mother is telling the truth and he couldn't have committed the murder."

"Wow, that is a big difference."

"How was your day?"

"My day was pretty good. I went out to lunch with my friends and ran a few errands."

"Who was at lunch?"

"Michelle and Allison. Why?"

"I was just curious. What is for dinner?"

"We are having enchiladas."

"That sounds good."

"Do you want to help?"

"Sure, I will help you," Tom said. "What do you want me to do?"

"Help me fill the tortillas."

"Okay, let me wash my hands."

"Here hold the tortilla open and I will put the filling in and you roll it."

"This is messy. You do this every time?"

"Yes. How else do you think that it gets done?"

"Magic?"

"Funny. Now we bake them for thirty minutes and then dinner is ready."

"That gives me enough time to watch a little bit of the news."

"I think that I will join you."

Tom and Karen went into the living room and settled into the couch to relax for a little bit. After about thirty minutes the oven bell went off.

"I need to go check on dinner."

Karen walked into the kitchen and turned on the light for the oven. She then looked through the window and saw that the cheese was melted and bubbling.

Karen hollered, "Dinner is ready! Will you please go and get the kids from upstairs?"

"I will go get them."

Tom walked up stairs to find both kids in Jeremy's room playing with his race track.

"Come on, kids, it's time for dinner. Wash your hands and go downstairs to the dining room."

Tom walked back down the stairs and into the kitchen. He walked over to wash his hands at the sink and stopped to give Karen a kiss as he passed by her at the stove. Karen was whipping up some refried beans and rice to serve with dinner.

Karen asked, "Can you put the enchiladas on the table so that I can carry over the beans and rice?"

"Yeah, no problem."

The kids came into the room and sat in their chairs, while Karen and Tom carried over dinner.

Tom asked, "Did you kids wash your hands?"

"Well, I did."

"Jeremy, did you wash your hands?"

"I rinsed them with water."

Tom said sternly, "Go wash your hands and use soap!"

"Okay, Daddy I will be right back."

Jeremy went running out of the room and came back a couple of minutes later.

"Anna, how did your spelling test go today?"

"I got a C plus on it."

"What happened?"

"I just don't spell good."

"You don't spell well. You will do better next time and look at it this way, you still passed."

Jeremy came running back to the table.

"I washed my hands this time, Daddy."

"That's good, chief. Anna, are you okay?"

"I just wish that I got a better grade."

"Well, next time we will study harder and you will do better, okay?"

"Will you help me next week?"

"Yes, I will set some time aside to help quiz you next week."

"Thank you, Daddy."

"You're welcome, princess," Tom said, "Jeremy, how did you do with your months?"

"I got all of them today!"

"Good job, buddy," Karen said. "What do you kids want to do tomorrow?"

Jeremy replied, "I want to go to the park."

"Yeah, going to the park sounds like fun."

"I was thinking that we could bar-b-que at home this weekend."

"That sounds good." Karen asked, "What do you want to bar-b-que?"

"I was thinking about just hot dogs and hamburgers. I thought that we could invite Mike over. What do you think?"

"That sounds good. I'll give him a call after dinner to see if he wants to come over."

"Is he seeing anyone?"

"I don't think so. Why, what are you up to?"

"Well, Allison isn't seeing anyone either and I thought that if I invite her and you invite him. We'll just see where it goes."

Tom said, "I don't want any part of this plan."

"Fine, just invite him. Then you're out of it."

"Okay, fine. I will call him."

"That is all that I ask."

"Let's get this mess cleaned up and I will give Mike a call."

Karen said, "Kids, please put your plates in the sink. Anna, help your brother."

The kids carried their plates over to the sink. Anna put her plate in first and then took the plate from her brother and put his in the sink too. Tom and Karen started to clear the rest of the food and dishes from the table.

Tom said, "I'll do the dishes if you put the food away."

"Deal. Kids, why don't you go play until bedtime? Please put on your pajamas."

Anna said, "Okay, Mommy. Oh, can I stay up later because it's not a school night?"

"Let me talk to your dad about it first and we will let you know."

"Okay, Mommy."

The kids ran off to play upstairs.

Tom said, "I guess since you want to do the bar-b-que you made your decision about the dog?"

"Yes, I have I been thinking that we could go get the dog in the morning and then have everyone over Sunday afternoon."

"So, you're saying yes to the dog?"

"I'm saying yes."

"That's great," Tom said. "This will be a great surprise for the kids."

"I think that this dog is just as much for you as for the kids."

"Yeah, maybe. I have wanted a dog for a while and now that we have the room and the kids are old enough, I don't see why we couldn't have one."

"It just seems that you really want this dog."

"It's a rare breed. It would be cool to have a rare breed like that."

"Call them in the morning to make sure that they still have dogs left, then we will head out there."

"That sounds good. I'll get up in the morning and call."

"Now you should be making another call."

"What call are you talking about?"

"You need to call Mike and invite him over Sunday."

"Oh yeah, that call. Okay, I will call right now. What time should I tell him?"

"I think that 2:30 pm should be a good time to have everyone show up."

Tom picked up the phone and dialed Mike's number.

"Hello, Tom."

"How did you know that it was me?"

"Caller ID. What's up?"

"Well, Karen had this idea to have a bar-b-que Sunday afternoon. She told me to invite you over."

Karen said in the background, "Don't tell him about Allison coming."

Tom whispered, "Okay, okay," while waving her off.

"Is she trying to set me up again?"

"I don't think so. We are just having some people over."

"Okay, I'll be there. Did she say yes to the dog?"

"She said yes, and we are going to get the dog tomorrow morning. As long as they still have puppies left."

"Did you take my advice, and just come out with it instead of tricking her?"

"Yes, I did."

"And it worked, didn't it?"

"Yes, it did. Do you want me to tell you that you were right?"

"That would be nice."

"Okay, you were right."

"Well, good luck at getting your dog tomorrow and I will see you Sunday afternoon. What time?"

"We were thinking around 2:30 pm."

"I will be there."

"Okay. I will see you Sunday."

Tom hung up the phone and walked over to Karen.

"He will be here, but he does suspect you of setting him up."

"As long as he comes that is all that matters. Now I need to call Allison."

Karen walked over picked up the phone and dialed Allison's phone number.

"Hello?"

"Hi, Allison."

"Hi. What's going on?"

"We are going to have a couple of people over for a bar-b-que Sunday and we were wondering if you would like to come?

"What time?"

"We were thinking at having everyone show up at around 2:30 pm. Just so that you know, Tom's partner is going to be there. The one that I told you about."

"I don't need a set-up. Wait, is he the cute one?"

"Yes, he is the cute one, but he already thinks that this is a set-up and Tom told him that it wasn't. I just hope that you guys hit it off."

"Yeah, me too. All right. I will see you Sunday."

"I will see you Sunday."

Karen hung up the phone and walked over to Tom.

"Okay, we are all set up for Sunday."

"Okay. Remember I don't have anything to do with this because I don't want to hear about it at work."

"Okay, okay. Hey, I need to talk about your daughter."

"What about my daughter?"

"Well she asked if she could stay up later because it's the weekend."

"I don't see why that would be a problem."

Karen asked, "Do you think that it is a good idea to let her stay up?"

"Well, I think that it would be a good trial run to see if she can handle a later bedtime. I think that she should be able to stay up later than her brother because she is after all two years older than him. I had an earlier bedtime than my older sister when I was a kid."

"I just don't know. I guess it's just because I was an only child."

"I say that we give her a shot and see if she can handle it."

"I will go with you on this but only because it's the weekend."

"Okay, how long should we let her stay up?"

"I would be comfortable with thirty extra minutes."

"I was thinking the same thing."

"Okay, then we will let her stay up until 8:30 pm."

"She asked you, so you should be the one to tell her."

"Oh, so I get to be the good guy this time?"

"You get to be the good guy sometimes."

"Yeah, sometimes."

"Do you want me to come up with you to put Jeremy to bed?" asked Tom. "He might be upset when he finds out that Anna gets to stay up later."

"That might be a good idea. He might take it better from you."

"That is going to be a change."

"What's that?"

"You get to be the good guy and I'm the bad guy."

They walked up the stairs to send Jeremy to bed and let Anna know that she could stay up later. They walked into Jeremy's room first.

Tom said, "Jeremy it's time for bed."

"But it's not a school night."

"I'll tell you what, when you get to be eight years old, we will let you stay up later on the weekends. Okay?"

"Okay. Wait, does that mean that Anna gets to stay up later because she is eight?"

"Yes, that is what that means."

Karen said, "Don't worry. The next two years are going to go by fast."

"Okay, Mommy."

Karen leaned over Jeremy and tucked him into bed nice and tight.

"Goodnight, buddy. I love you."

"Goodnight, Mommy. I love you too."

"Goodnight, chief. I love you."

"Goodnight, Daddy. I love you too."

Tom and Karen left Jeremy's room and walked over to Anna's room.

"Do I have to go to bed now?"

Karen declared, "You have another half an hour."

"Really?"

"Yeah, really," Karen said. "We will be back up in thirty minutes to tuck you into bed."

"Okay, Mommy. Thank you."

"You're welcome, honey bear."

Tom and Karen walked out of Anna's room and back down the stairs. They settled into the couch to watch a little TV for the evening.

Karen asked, "What do you want to watch tonight?"

"How about one of your Hallmark movies?"

"But you don't like those movies."

"But you do, and I wanted to be nice tonight. Besides, you said yes to the dog."

"Thank you."

"You're welcome."

They turned on the movie and started it. They watched about thirty minutes of it and then put it on pause. Then they walked up the stairs and found Anna in her bedroom playing with her dolls.

"Anna, it's time for bed."

"Okay, Mommy I will go to bed."

Karen walked over and gave her a kiss on the forehead.

"Goodnight, honey bear. I love you."

"Goodnight, Mommy. I love you too."

"Goodnight, princess. I love you."

"Goodnight, Daddy. I love you too."

Tom and Karen left Anna's room and walked back down the stairs. They settled down onto the couch to watch the rest of their movie. When the movie ended, they started to stir again.

Karen said, "It's been a long day, so I think that I'm going to go to bed."

"I think that I'm ready for bed as well. Why don't you head up? I will shut everything down. Then I will be up."

"Sounds good to me."

Karen headed up to bed while Tom started to check the doors and turn off the lights. Then Tom headed upstairs to find Karen already changed and in bed.

"I guess you didn't waste any time."

"I'm tired. I told you that I was ready to go to sleep."

"Well, I'm going to join you in a minute."

Tom walked into the bathroom to brush his teeth and then he headed to bed to find Karen already asleep. He climbed into bed and drifted off to sleep while thinking how surprised the kids would be when they found out that they were going to get to take home a dog tomorrow.

SATURDAY

Tom woke up to find that Karen was already up and downstairs. Tom walked down the stairs and ran into the smell of bacon and coffee.

Tom said, "I woke up into a dream."

"What do you mean?"

"Coffee and bacon. The smell is filling the house and I love it."

"I did it just for you."

"You did?"

"No, it's just that I'm fixing bacon for breakfast for the kids."

"And the coffee?"

"I wanted some."

"And here I thought that I was special."

"See what you get for thinking. No, I was kidding. You are special."

"Good. You were making me feel bad."

"You have always been special to me. Do you want some breakfast?"

"What are you making besides bacon?"

"I'm going to make French toast. Would you like some?"

"That sounds good, Yeah I'll have some. Thank you."

"Not a problem, I enjoy cooking for my family. Hey, did you make that call yet?"

"Not yet."

"Don't you think you should?"

"Yeah I'll do that now."

Tom picked up the phone and dialed the number for the ranch. A woman answered the phone.

"Hello?"

"Hi, my name is Tom and I was wondering if you were the people that had those Hangin' Tree Cattle Dog puppies?"

"Yes, we are."

"Do you still have any left?"

"Yes, we have two male dogs and one female left."

"How much?"

"$300 for each of the males and $500 for the female."

"Can we reserve a dog? We will be out to pick it up later this morning and we will be bringing cash."

"A dog is yours. Do you want a male or a female?"

"I believe that we will take a male dog."

"You just have to pick out which one that you want."

"Great. We will see you in a few hours."

"Okay, we will see you then. But when you get here the house is a little tricky to get to."

"How tricky?"

"When you get to the ranch, we live about three and a half miles off the road. You will drive through the white gate across the cattle catcher," she said. "Then you will come to a gate about a half a mile in. You will need to drive through that gate, be sure to close it behind you or the cattle will get out. Then you will drive another two and a half miles and you will come to another gate. You will need to drive through that gate and again be sure to close it behind you again so that we can keep the cattle contained. Then it's another half of a mile to the house."

"Okay, got it."

"Do you know about what time we can expect you?"

"I figure that we should be there at between 12 to 12:30 pm."

"Okay, we will see you then."

"Okay, bye."

Tom hung up the phone and walked back into the kitchen.

"They have three dogs left, two males and one female. They are holding one of the males for us."

"That's great. Why did you say that we would take a male? I know that you prefer female dogs."

"The female dog costs more than the male dogs."

"Oh okay. Is there something else bothering you?"

"I want to ask you a question, but I don't want you to get mad over it."

"What is it?" Karen asked. "I promise that I won't get mad."

"Have you put any more thought into the idea of going back to work now that Jeremy is almost in the first grade?"

"I have thought about it, but I think that I enjoy being home for the kids when they get home from school. Why? Do you think that I should be going back to work?"

"I think that you should do what you want to do. If you think that you should go back to work, then I think that you should go back to work but if you think that you should be home with the kids then you should be at home."

"I'll take that as you think that I should go back to work because that is what you said first."

"How long do we have to be married for you to realize that you can't read me that way?"

"Well, wouldn't you like to have the extra income?"

"Yes, the extra income would be nice. Then we could be able to afford more extras..."

"See, you want the extra income."

"No, that isn't what I was saying. You didn't let me finish. I really think that I would rather you be home for the kids so that they are raised by us and not a day care or after school program."

"Are you sure?" Karen asked. "What about the extra money?"

"We do just fine now. We even have the money to take a vacation once a year. When we really need you to go back to work is when they are more independent in high school or at the latest college to help pay for it."

"I will go back to work if you want me to."

"I know but I would really much rather you stay at home to raise the kids."

"Then that's what I will do. I'm going to stay at home. Is that all you wanted to talk to me about? I need to call the kids for breakfast."

"Yes, that was it."

"Kids! Breakfast is on the table."

The kids came running in and sat down at the table.

Karen asked, "Did you two wash your hands?"

"No, neither did Jeremy."

"Mommy, she is being a tattle-tale!"

"Maybe so, but I don't want you to get sick, so go wash your hands anyway."

"Okay, Mommy, I will."

Both kids got up and went into the downstairs bathroom to wash their hands. Then they came back to their seats.

"Are your hands clean?"

Both kids said, "Yes, Mommy."

"How many pieces of toast and bacon do you want, Anna?"

"Two of each, Mommy."

"How many pieces of toast and bacon do you want, Jeremy?"

"Two of each, Mommy."

Anna asked, "Daddy, can we go to the park today?"

"No, princess, we are going to go for a road trip today."

"Okay, why can't we stop at a park while we are driving?"

"No, princess, we are going to take a family drive through the country."

"But I want to go to the park!"

"I want to go to the park too!"

"If you don't watch your tone the only place that you will be going is your room for the rest of the day with no toys."

Anna replied, "I'm sorry, Daddy."

"I'm sorry too, Daddy."

"It's okay. We will go to the park next weekend."

"Okay, thank you."

"You're welcome."

"After breakfast we are going to be taking a long drive into the county, so if you want something to do in the car you had better take it with you."

Karen said, "I'm going to take a few sandwiches to eat in the car."

"That's a good idea because we may get hungry and we aren't going to have time to stop."

"How long of a drive do you think that we are going to be taking?"

"We shouldn't be gone longer than four to five hours."

Karen said, "Okay, kids. Take your plates to the sink."

"We are leaving in about an hour so make sure that you get whatever you want to do in the car and use the bathroom right before we leave."

"Do you want to clear the table and do the dishes while I make up a lunch to take with us?"

"That's a good idea. I'll get started."

Tom started to clear the table and put stuff away. Karen got out the bread, lunch meat mayonnaise, and lettuce to make sandwiches for their lunch.

"What kind of sandwich do you want?"

"I would love a roast beef sandwich, thank you. What are you going to make for the kids?"

"I'm going to make the kids ham sandwiches and myself a turkey sandwich."

"They will like that. I can't wait to see their faces when we tell them that we are taking the dog home."

"Yeah, it's going to be priceless."

"I think that we should take the camera."

"I think that is a good idea."

Tom yelled, "Hey kids, we are leaving in about fifteen minutes so get your stuff down here and use the bathroom."

Anna asked, "Even if we don't have to go?"

"Yes, even if you don't have to. You might be surprised."

"Okay."

The kids came running down the stairs about ten minutes later.

Jeremy said, "Mommy, where are we going?"

"We are going for a drive in the country."

Tom said, "Okay, kids, let's all get into the car so that we can get going."

Everyone headed out of the door.

"Honey, could you get the cooler? It has the sandwiches and drinks in there."

"Yeah, I got it."

Everyone climbed into the car. Tom started the car and backed out of the driveway.

Anna asked, "Daddy, where are we going?"

Karen said, "I told you we are going for a drive."

"Okay, Mommy, I just thought that Daddy would know since he is driving."

"Daddy and I do know but it's a surprise for you so please stop asking."

"Okay, Mommy. How long will it take to get there?"

"A couple of hours."

"Wow, that's a long time."

"Yes, it is. That is why you brought toys and we can play car games."

"What kind of car games?"

"Well there is the 'License Plate' game, a game that I played when I was a kid called 'Bug' that was always a fun one. There is also one called ABC license plate game and Counting Cows."

"What are they?"

"The 'License Plate' game is when you try to spot a license plate from different states until you have named all of the states at the end of the game. The one that has found the most states wins."

"What are the other games?"

"The game 'Bug' is when you see a Volkswagen Bug you call it first and that is one point if you see a van first that is worth two points. If you see an emergency vehicle, they are worth ten points and buses are also worth ten points. When you get to where you're going, or you just get tired of playing then the person with the most points wins. Does that sound like something that you want to play?"

"How do you play the ABC License Plate game?"

"The ABC License Plate game is when you say the ABCs by finding the letters in a license plate and the first one that gets the letter Z wins after going in order. You can only use one letter per license plate."

"What's the Counting Cows game?

"The Counting Cows game is when you count as many cows as you can but if you drive past a cemetery you lose them all and you start counting again."

Jeremy said, "I want to play the ABC game!"

"I want to play the 'Bug' game!"

"Anna, could we please play the ABC License Plate game? It would really help your brother reinforce his ABCs."

"I guess we can play the ABC game. When do we start?"

"How about now?"

"Okay, there is an A."

Tom piped up and said, "There's my A."

Anna asked, "You're playing, Daddy?"

"Yeah, just because I'm driving doesn't mean that I can't play."

Jeremy said, "There's an A and there's a B."

"That's not fair. I wasn't paying attention."

Karen responded, "Then pay attention. It's fair."

Jeremy said, "There is a C."

Tom said, "There is a B."

Karen said, "There is my A and there is my B."

Anna said, "There is my B and there is a C. This is kind of fun."

Karen replied, "It also passes the time."

Jeremy declared, "Mommy, I have to go potty."

Tom asked, "Did you go before we left?"

"Yes, Daddy, I swear."

"Okay, we will stop at the next gas station. Can you hold it?"

"I will try."

"Everyone look for a place to stop."

Anna exclaimed, "There is a gas station, Daddy."

"It will be just a few more minutes, Jeremy. Just hold on."

"Okay, Daddy, I'm trying."

Tom pulled into the driveway and parked in the parking lot. The parking lot was rather large. There was a big open area behind and to the side of the building to accommodate semi-trucks because it was the last station for ninety-seven miles according to the sign on the street. There were gas pumps in front with a convenience store behind them. Inside there was an island with a register on either side. There were all kinds of little impulse buys all around the registers. On the left side of the island there were aisles with food and supplies on the shelves. On the right side there were tables to sit at to eat and rest. In the back there was a food counter with all kinds of things to eat from fried chicken to pizza. At the right back corner was where you got the fountain drinks and in the left back corner in the restroom. They pulled into the gas island.

"I think that I should go ahead and get gas just to make sure that we don't run out here."

"That's probably a good idea. Come on, kids, let's go."

"But I don't have to go."

"It won't hurt you to try."

"Okay, I will try."

Tom got out and started to pump the gas while the others went into the store to use the restroom.

Anna said, "Hey look, Mommy. They have pizza. Could we get one?"

"No, we have sandwiches in the car, remember?"

"Okay."

"You need to go in first, Jeremy. Is there anything that you need help with?"

"No, Mommy, I got it."

Jeremy walked into the bathroom and closed the door.

When Jeremy walked out, he said, "I feel better."

"That's good. Okay, Anna, it's your turn."

"Okay, Mommy, but I'm telling you I don't have to go."

"Just try."

With that, the door shut with Anna inside.

"Mommy, can I have a candy bar?"

"We'll see. I don't know."

Karen texted Tom and asked, "They want a candy bar. What do you think?"

He texted back, "They are going to be wound up with the dog anyway, so I don't think that it matters. Go ahead and let them have one. Please get me a Reese's Peanut Butter Cup."

"Jeremy, you can go ahead and pick out a candy bar but stay where I can see you, okay?"

"Okay."

Jeremy went over to the candy aisle and picked out a Butterfinger candy bar. Anna came out of the bathroom and saw that Jeremy had a candy bar.

"I want one!"

"Did you go?"

"Yes, I went."

"See I told you, you should always try when you get the chance."

"Okay, Mommy."

"Go ahead and pick out a candy bar."

"Thank you."

"You're welcome, honey bear."

Anna picked out a Baby Ruth candy bar. Karen picked up a Reese's Peanut Butter Cup for Tom and a Mounds Bar for herself.

"I got one, Mommy."

"Come on, kids. Let's get checked out and headed to out."

Karen and the kids headed over to the register to check out.

"Did you find everything that you needed?"

"Yes, we did. Come on, kids, put your candy bars on the counter so the nice lady can ring them up."

The kids put their candy bars on the counter and the cashier scanned them.

"Your total is $6.48."

Karen handed the cashier a ten.

"Your change is $3.52. Thank you and have a wonderful day."

"Thank you and you have a wonderful day too."

Karen and the kids walked back out to the car where Tom was done pumping gas.

Tom said, "Time to get back on the road."

Everyone got back into the car.

Karen said, "Seatbelts on, everyone."

Jeremy asked, "Can we have our candy bars?"

Tom said, "No, we are going to have lunch soon. You can have it after lunch."

Karen asked, "How much further is it?"

"According to the GPS we are about thirty miles away."

"That isn't far, maybe I will get out the sandwiches now so that it's done before—well, you know."

"Yeah, that's a good idea."

"Do you want to pull over somewhere?"

"There isn't any place to pull over, so we'll have to eat in the car."

"Anna, reach into the back and get the sandwiches."

"Mommy, I can't lift the cooler."

"Don't worry about it. Just open it up and get the sandwiches out."

"Okay, who gets which sandwich?"

"Your dad gets the roast beef, I get the turkey and you guys get ham sandwiches."

"Okay, Mommy, here you go."

"Thank you, honey bear."

Everybody enjoyed their sandwich and ate without talking much.

Karen said, "Look, there are some deer. You don't see them in the city."

Anna said, "That's cool."

"Wow, awesome."

Tom said, "I think that this is it up here."

"Are you sure?"

"Yeah, It's the white gate with a cattle catcher. I'm going to turn in here."

"Okay."

They drove for about a half of a mile and found a gate.

"Now I'm sure that this is the right place because this is right where the second gate is supposed to be."

"I'll get out and get the gate."

"Okay but wait until I pull through because you have to close the gate behind us too."

"Okay."

Karen got out of the car and opened the gate. Then Tom pulled through the gate and Karen closed it behind him. Then she got back into the car. As they drove through the ranch there were a lot of cows.

"Hey, kids," Karen said. "Look at all the cows."

Jeremy replied, "There are a lot of them."

"Yeah there are."

They came up to the next gate about two and a half miles in.

"I'm guessing that I need to close this gate behind us too."

"Yes, please and thank you."

Karen got back out of the car and opened the gate while Tom pulled through. Then Karen closed the gate and got back into the car.

"How many more gates are there?"

"There shouldn't be any more. The house should be next in about a half of a mile."

They drove for a few minutes and the house came into view. It was a white farm house. The outside looked like a log cabin with a large porch that had a porch swing on the end of it. It was two story with an attic. Behind the house was a large yard with green grass and a tree in the middle of the yard providing lots of shade. Then there was a riding arena. It was a large white metal building with large doors on the side of it. Looking through the doors you could see a sitting area just inside to the right. Off that building there was a round pen situated between the arena and the barn. The barn was a large red building with white trim. There was a large barn door to be able to move horses in and out of the barn next to a standard-sized house door for people to enter and exit. There were corrals along the outside of the barn for horses to be able to be inside or out. On the outside of the barn there were two dog pens. One housed the dad dog of all the puppies and the other housed all the puppies that haven't been picked up by their new owners yet.

Jeremy asked, "Dad, what are we doing here?"

"I just need to talk to these people for a minute."

Tom parked the car and got out. A man and woman walked up to him.

"Hi, I'm Tom."

"Hello, I'm Jack and this is my wife Linda. I understand that you're interested in our last two dogs?"

"Yes—wait, I thought that there were three."

He looked down to see a little black dog sniffing at his leg. There was another white one running across the yard. The black dog was almost all black. It had a little white on two of its toes, some dark brown around its mouth and a single white hair on the back of his neck. The white dog was all white except on his rump and around his right eye there was blue marled. He had a pink nose and baby blue eyes.

"There were three, but we just sold the female over the phone about an hour ago."

"Oh, okay. Is this them?"

"Yes, these two are the ones available. Why is your family still in the car?"

"The kids still don't know why we are here."

Tom motioned for everyone to get out. Karen opened her car door and stepped out of the car. Then she opened the back door.

Karen said, "Come on, kids, get out of the car."

The kids both climbed out of the car and immediately found the puppy running around at their feet.

"This is my wife Karen and our kids Anna and Jeremy."

"Hi, nice to meet you."

Anna asked, "Mommy, can we play with the puppies?"

"Yes, you can."

Tom asked, "Do you like the puppies?"

Anna and Jeremy both said, "Yes."

"Which one is your favorite?"

Anna said, "I like the black one."

"The white one in my favorite."

Tom turned to Karen and asked, "What do you want to do?"

"I don't know. We didn't plan on this."

"What if we took both?"

"That is a lot of work for me."

"That is why it's your choice."

"I hate when you put everything on me."

"Do you want me to make the decision?"

"No, because I know what you would say."

"What would I say?"

"You would say let's take them both."

"Well, what are you saying?"

"So, my options are to disappoint one of my children or take home two dogs."

"Yeah, that is what you have to decide."

"Do you even have six hundred dollars on you?"

"I don't know. Let me look."

Tom looked in his wallet and found five hundred and twenty dollars.

"All I have is five hundred and twenty so if you don't have eighty then we can only take home one dog."

Karen got her purse out of the car and looked inside her wallet. There was exactly eighty dollars inside.

"I have eighty dollars exactly."

"Does this mean that we are going to take both dogs?"

"After all that to find enough money I think that we have to."

"Besides that, having them together will make the transition easier for them."

"True. I guess we are taking them both."

"Hey Jack, how would you feel about getting rid of both dogs?"

"That sounds good to me."

"Okay, here is six hundred."

"Thank you."

"Come on kids, we are leaving," Tom said.

Both kids said, "We don't want to go. We want to play with the puppies."

"Then bring the puppies with you."

Anna replied, "Really? Both?"

"Yes, you each get your own dog. But you must learn to take care of it. Feed it, water it and train it."

"I will, I promise."

"You too, Jeremy."

"I will."

"All right, put your dog in the car and get in. Seatbelts please!"

Tom and Karen got into the car as well. They started the car and drove back out of the driveway. The kids were playing with their puppies.

Karen said, "Now you have to think of a name for your dogs."

"I don't know what to name him," Anna said. "Daddy, what would you name him?"

Tom said, "How about Rover?"

"I don't like that. I want something that is a real name."

Karen asked, "What do you mean by a real name?"

"Like my name but I want a boy's name."

"So not like Sampson?" Tom asked.

"No."

"Okay, something like Harry, Jerry, or Jake?"

"Jake, I like Jake."

Karen said, "Jake is a good name."

"I'm going to name you Jake. Hi, Jake."

"What about your puppy, Jeremy?"

"Mine is easy. I'm going to name him Blue."

"Why Blue? Is it because of the blue around his eye and on his rump?"

"No, it's because of his blue eyes. They are pretty."

"Yes, they are. I think that is the perfect name for him."

"Blue, that is your name. What do you think of it?"

The puppies licked the kids and wagged their tails. The kids played with their puppies until the halfway point on the way home. It got quiet in the back seat, so Karen looked back to find all four of them asleep in the seat.

Karen said, "They are all asleep."

"Really? Even the puppies?"

"Yeah, the kids are asleep in their car seats and the puppies are curled up together on the seat in between the kids. They are so cute."

"Are you regretting getting both puppies?"

"After seeing them together like they are, I definitely do not regret getting both. I think that the kids are going to sleep like babies tonight."

"Yeah, they have had a big day. We need to stop by the hardware store on the way home."

"Why?"

"I want to get a dog door for the sliding glass door. I'm not going to have the dogs need to get out and have no one paying attention."

"You know that they are still puppies and they will have accidents in the house, especially at first."

"I know but this will still help, especially later as they get older."

"I don't want to have a back door that doesn't lock."

"No, they do lock. The only problem with them is they take away the space to walk through the door, but I think that they are worth it. They will keep some of the messes down."

"Okay. What do they cost?"

"I looked it up online last night and they run about two hundred dollars."

"Isn't that expensive?"

"Not for what you get. Trust me, they look nice. If you want later, we could put a door in the wall."

"Let's see how this one works out first."

Tom drove into the driveway of the hardware store. It was a warehouse store with a rather large parking lot for a large building. There was a parking spot about halfway back from the store.

"I'm just going to run in so that we don't have to wake up the kids."

Tom got out of the car and closed the door softly to keep from waking up the kids. As he walked into the store, he saw a customer service counter to the right and aisles of appliances, plumbing and construction hardware in front and to the left of him. Tom walked over to the customer service counter and waited in line. He was next.

"Can I help you?"

"Yes, I'm looking for a pet door for a sliding glass patio door. Could you tell me where I can find it?"

"Yes, it would be in the doors and windows area. Aisle number 22."

"Okay, thank you."

Tom walked away toward the center of the store in the back where the doors and windows area was. He walked all around the area and couldn't find the pet doors anywhere. Then he saw an employee and walked over to him.

"Can you help me?"

"Sure. What do you need?"

"I'm looking for a pet door that goes into the sliding glass door. Do you know where I can find one?"

"I know right where they are if you come with me, I'll show you."

Tom followed the employee over two aisles and about halfway down on the left. There were several different kinds.

"Is there anything else that I can help you with?"

"No, that is it, thank you."

Tom looked at all the options and chose one. Then he headed for the checkout. He found a lane that was open with no waiting.

"Did you find everything that you need?"

"Yes, I finally found it."

"That will be $267.84."

Tom placed his credit card into the card reader. Pressed OK on the total. Then he signed the screen.

"Thank you, have a nice day."

"Thank you, you too."

Tom walked out to the car to find his kids awake and playing with the puppies. He tried to put the pet door into the trunk of the car, but it was too long. So, he found a bungee cord in the trunk to fasten it down. He then got back into the car and started it up.

"Did you find what you were looking for?"

"Yeah, eventually. There were a lot of them."

"What do you mean?"

"They ranged from $225 to $600."

"Please tell me that you didn't get the $600 one."

"No, I got the one that cost about $250 because it has an air flap to seal the sides to help with energy bills."

"Okay, I can accept that. That is only $50 more than what you said earlier."

"With tax it cost about $268. I just put it on the credit card."

They drove up to the house.

"Hey kids, let's show Jake and Blue their new home."

"Okay, Daddy, come on. Jake, I'm going to show you your new room. You have to share with me."

"Blue, you will be sharing with me."

Karen asked, "Are you going to install that pet door today?"

"Yes, I'm going to put it in right away and then introduce it to the puppies."

They got out of the car and headed up to the door, except for Tom, who walked to the back of the car and got out the pet door and walked in. Tom opened the pet door box and pulled it out.

"How complicated is it to put together?"

"It looks like you just set it in place."

Tom opened the door and slid down the compression sleeve and then let it go when it was in place. Then he shook it to make sure that it was secure.

"It looks like that is it."

"Wow, that was simple."

Tom opened the pet door and then started to look for the puppies.

"Kids bring your puppies down here," bellowed Tom.

The kids come walking in struggling to carry their respective puppies.

Anna asked, "What do you need, Daddy?"

"I want to put your dogs outside and see if they can figure out how to get back in on their own through the dog door. So, put them outside."

As he opened the door, the kids took their puppies outside and put them down. They immediately went to the bathroom.

"Hurry up, kids. Get in here."

He shut the door behind the kids as they entered the house.

"Now I want you to put the dogs outside every couple of hours to get them trained to go outside and not in the house. Do you know what to do when they go in the house?"

Anna answered, "Yeah. If they go in the house give them a swat on the rear."

"No, you push their nose down to it and tell them sternly 'No,' then you take them outside."

"What does sternly mean?"

"You know how your mom and I talk to you when you're in trouble?"

"Yeah, I hate that voice. It always makes me feel bad about myself."

"It's supposed to, and it will work for them too."

"Okay, Daddy."

"Do you understand, Jeremy?"

"Yes, Daddy."

"Let me be clear. You are not to hit them, okay?"

Both said, "Okay, Daddy, we won't."

Anna asked, "What do we do about the mess?"

"If and when you find one, then get me. If you don't know who it then don't punish either of them. You don't like getting trouble for something that you didn't do, do you?"

"Okay, Daddy. I understand. Look, they are coming in through the pet door."

"Yes, here they come. They are pretty smart dogs."

"Come on, Jake. Come on, boy. That's it."

"Come on, Blue," Jeremy said. "You're a good boy."

"Okay, kids. Go and play until dinner."

"Okay. Come on, Jeremy, let's take the puppies upstairs."

"Okay."

Tom walked into the kitchen where Karen was preparing dinner.

"You made those kids' day by getting both dogs. They are so happy with them."

"Yeah, they are pretty happy, aren't they?"

"Hey, what's for dinner?"

"You didn't see the bird on top of the oven? We are having baked whole chicken with stuffing, green beans and dinner rolls."

"Wow, that sounds really good. What made you think of making such an elaborate meal after the day that we had?"

"Well, after the day of traveling that we had I figured that everyone could use a good meal. Besides, it's going to take over an hour to cook so I can relax for a little while now."

"Do you want to watch TV while you take your break?"

"No, I want to sit on the couch, cuddle up with you and fall asleep while you watch TV so that you can wake me up in an hour."

"Okay, you have a deal."

Tom and Karen walked over to the couch and sat down. Karen grabbed a blanket and cuddled up to Tom on the couch. Within minutes she was asleep. Tom decided to set the alarm on his phone for one hour just in case because he was also exhausted. A few minutes after Karen fell asleep, Tom started to drift off. What seemed like a few minutes later the alarm went off and Tom woke up. He then started to wake up Karen.

"Karen, Karen, wake up. It's time to finish dinner."

Karen sleepily said, "What?"

"It's been an hour. It's time to finish up dinner."

"Okay, I'm up."

Karen stood up slowly, stretching toward the ceiling and yawning. She started to walk to the kitchen.

"Tom, why don't you help me with dinner? It will make it easier if we do it together."

"You mean easier for you."

"Don't you want to make things easier for me?"

"I guess that is what they say love is all about."

"Yes, it is, and you love me, so get your butt in here."

"Yes, dear."

Tom walked in the kitchen and washed his hands. On his way into the kitchen he stopped and kissed his wife on the cheek.

"What would you like me to do?"

"I thought that you could do the stuffing. Do you think that you can handle that?"

"I think that I can handle that."

Tom took the box of stuffing and followed the directions on it.

Tom hollered, "Kids, bring your puppies down here."

The kids come down the stairs with the puppies in tow.

"Take your dogs outside and go to the far side of the yard and let them walk back on their own. Then go wash your hands for dinner."

Jeremy said, "Okay, Daddy."

"We will be right back."

Tom helped put the chicken on a meat plate and then carried it over to the table. Karen grabbed the green beans and the stuffing and carried them over to the table. The kids came back into the dining room and sat down at their chairs.

Tom asked, "Anna, what kind of meat do you want?"

"I want a leg."

Tom cut off one of the legs of the chicken and gave it to Anna.

"Jeremy, what kind do you want?"

"I want the breast."

Tom cut of a slice of the breast for Jeremy and gave it to him.

"Okay, sweetie, what would you like?"

"I would like the other leg and a wing."

"I'll take the thigh and the other wing."

Tom then cut off the other leg, a thigh, and both wings. Tom then sat down to eat.

"So how are you kids getting along with the puppies?" Tom asked.

"Jake is the best puppy! He can already sit when I tell him to."

"What about you, Jeremy? How are you getting along with your puppy?"

"He keeps trying to run off with everything."

"I guess that you had better keep your room picked up then."

"I think that we all had better keep everything picked up around the house," Karen said. "We also need to keep an eye on their chewing. They are going to chew on everything."

Anna said, "They are coming in again."

Tom said, "That's good. Hopefully they will learn to go out through the door too. After dinner I want you kids to push your dogs through the door from this side. They will just come right back in but that is okay. The objective is to let them know that the door works both ways."

"Okay. I'll do that as soon as I get done eating."

"Sweetie, this chicken is really good. Did you do something different?"

"You know how I usually rub the outside of the chicken with herbs and spices?"

"Yeah, it usually makes the skin taste delicious."

"Well, I wanted to carry that taste to inside the chicken too. So, I mixed the herbs and spices in with soft butter and used my injector to inject the mixture into the meat of the bird. As the butter melted it mixed in with the natural juices of the meat, carrying the flavor with it."

"It was a good idea. I can taste the flavor throughout the chicken. It is exceptional."

"Thank you."

Anna said, "Yeah, it is really good, Mommy."

"Yeah, it's good."

"Well, thank you."

"Now let me help get this cleaned up," Tom said. "I'll start to do the dishes if you will clear the table and put the food away."

"Okay, sounds like a deal. Kids, take your plates over to the sink."

Both kids said, "Okay, Mommy."

"Don't forget about putting your dogs through the pet door from this side. Then you need to go put your pajamas on."

Both kids said, "Okay, Daddy."

"Don't forget, Daddy, I get to stay up later because it's the weekend."

"I know, princess. I didn't forget."

The kids went and found their dogs and put them through the pet door and the dogs came back in right away. Then they ran off to put on their pajamas. Tom started to do the dishes while Karen put away the food and wiped down the table.

Tom said, "It was one long day, wasn't it?"

"Yes, it was and I'm really happy that it's almost over."

"I'm guessing that you want to go to bed early, don't you?"

"I would like to at least not have you get upset with me when I fall asleep on the couch."

They finished doing the dishes and went over to the couch.

Tom yelled, "Kids, it's time to take the dogs outside again."

The kids came down the stairs with their dogs.

Tom said, "Hey, stop! Where are your slippers?"

Anna said, "We were just going to put them through the door."

"No, you have to take them to the far side of the yard, otherwise they will just come back in and go in the house. We don't want that, so go put on your slippers."

The kids went back upstairs to get their slippers. When they came back down the stairs the puppies followed them up and back down. They then took the dogs outside and kept them out there for a few minutes.

"Did the puppies go while they were outside?"

Anna said, "Yes they did."

"Okay, now I want you to take them out one more time before Jeremy goes to bed. Then I want you, Anna, to take them both out before you go to bed. Okay?"

"Okay, I will."

"Those kids are so happy to have those dogs."

Then he looked down to find Karen asleep lying up against his shoulder again. So, he turned on the TV and fell asleep too. When Tom woke up, he found that it was 9 pm. He woke up Karen.

"Karen, Karen, we have to put the kids to bed."

"What time is it?"

"It's 9 o'clock."

"They are still up?"

"Yes, I fell asleep too."

Tom and Karen walked up the stairs to find Anna still awake and Jeremy lying on his floor asleep.

Tom said, "Anna it's time for bed. You need to take out the dogs and then get into bed."

"I will get them now."

Tom walked into Jeremy's room and picked him up off the floor and put him into bed. He kissed him on the forehead and pulled the blankets up over him.

"Goodnight, chief. I love you."

Karen bent down and kissed him on the forehead.

"Goodnight, buddy. I love you."

About then Anna came back up the stairs.

Tom asked, "Did the puppies go?"

"Yes, they did, they went both ways."

"That's good. Now it's time for you to get into bed. It's past your bedtime."

"Okay, Daddy."

Anna climbed into bed and pulled her blankets up. Then she called Jake onto the bed with her.

Karen said, "Anna I don't think that he can jump that high yet."

"Could you pick him up and put him up here? Please?"

"Okay, here we go."

Karen bent down and picked up Jake and put him into bed with Anna.

Tom said, "I'll go put Blue into bed with Jeremy. I'm sure that he would enjoy waking up to him if he is still there when he wakes up."

Tom walked over to Jeremy's room and put Blue up into Jeremy's bed. He went right to Jeremy and curled up right next to him. Tom then walked back to Anna's room. He got back just as Karen bent down and kissed Anna on the forehead.

"Goodnight, honey bear. I love you."

"Goodnight, Mommy. I love you too."

Tom walked over and bent down and kissed Anna on the forehead.

"Goodnight, princess. I love you."

"Goodnight, Daddy. I love you."

Tom and Karen walked out of the room and turned off the light. When they left Jake was curled up right next to Anna's leg. They walked back down the stairs and sat on the couch.

Tom said, "I figure we can watch another hour of TV and Anna should be asleep by then. Then we can go to bed. What do you think?"

"That sounds like a plan. You how I hate to go to bed before the kids are asleep."

"I know. That is why I suggested it."

They went downstairs and sat back down on the couch.

"What would you like to watch?" Tom asked.

"Don't we have one of those cooking shows recorded?"

"Yes, I think so. You want to watch one of those?"

"Yeah, that sounds good."

"Okay, I'll turn it on."

Once it was over it was about 10 o'clock and Tom turned off the TV.

"I think that the kids are now both asleep. Do you want to shut everything down and then we can go up and check on the kids?"

"That's a good idea."

Tom and Karen checked all the locks and turned off all the lights. Then they headed upstairs. They stopped by Anna's room first to find her fast asleep cuddled up with Jake. Then they went to Jeremy's room to find him sleeping with Blue right by his side. They then walked into their room and closed the door.

Karen said, "I have to say, it's really nice to see the kids so happy."

"Yes, it is. So how tired are you?"

"Why, what are you getting at?"

"You know what I'm getting at."

As Tom pulled her closer to him, she reached up and kissed him passionately.

Sunday

The next morning, they woke up together.

Karen said, "I really enjoyed last night."

"I did too."

"I should hope so."

Tom smiled. "I heard the kids up, so we should get up too."

"Saved by the kids! Lucky you. Come on, let's get up."

Tom and Karen put on their robes and walked down the stairs to find both kids in front of the TV watching cartoons.

Tom asked, "Where are the dogs?"

"We took them outside," Anna said. "They are still there."

"That's good, good job."

Tom followed Karen into the kitchen to get some coffee.

Karen asked, "Do you kids want some breakfast?"

Anna said, "Yes please."

"What do you want?"

"Pancakes."

"Yeah pancakes."

"Do you want to go take your shower before breakfast and I will shower afterward."

"Sounds good."

Tom walked back upstairs to take a shower. When he came back down showered and dressed for the day, he found breakfast being put out on the table.

Tom said, "It looks good, sweetie."

"Thank you, honey. Come on, kids, come eat."

Everybody came in and sat down at the table to eat.

Karen asked, "Jeremy, how many pancakes do you want?"

"I want two."

"Okay, here are your two. Anna, how many pancakes for you?"

"I want three."

"Do you think you will be able to eat three?"

"Yes, I can."

"Okay, if you think that you can eat them. Here you go."

"Thank you, Mommy."

"How many do you want, honey?"

"I'll take three."

"And I will take three as well."

"These are good. You added something to it, didn't you?" Tom asked.

"Yes, I added cinnamon to the batter."

"Well, it's excellent."

"Did you go out to the freezer and get out the hamburger and hot dogs out for the bar-b-que?"

"No, but I will right after breakfast. Have you kids started to train your dogs yet?"

Anna said, "I told you last night that Jake can already sit."

"Yes, what I meant to say is have you been able to teach him anything else?"

"No, but we are working on it."

"What about you, Jeremy?"

"Blue is a little harder to train."

"Keep working at it. You will get there. I am proud of you both because of how you have both taken responsibility for your dogs."

Both said, "Thank you, Daddy."

Karen asked, "Has anyone seen my slipper? When I woke up and came downstairs, I found one but the other one was gone."

"Oh yeah, I found it this morning in my room. I think Blue took it in the middle of the night."

"Anna, we have to finish your solar system project tonight."

"I know."

"You don't sound like you want to do it."

"Mommy, it's homework, I don't ever want to do homework."

"This will be fun, you'll see. Maybe we can even get your dad to help."

"Will you help, Daddy?"

"Yes, I will help. It will be fun. I think that the whole family can take part in this project. What do you say, Jeremy?"

"I guess I can help."

"You will help. It will be a fun family project."

"I guess it won't be so bad if everyone helps."

Karen said, "There is more if anybody is still hungry."

"I think that I will have one more. They are really good."

Anna responded, "I think that I took too much. I'm stuffed."

"But Anna, you still have a quarter of your pancakes left."

"I know, Mommy. I'm sorry."

"It's okay, honey bear. You don't know until you try. There isn't anything to be sorry for."

"What about you, Jeremy? Would you like to have more?"

"No, I'm full. Thank you, Mommy."

"You're welcome, buddy."

Tom said, "Now I have eaten too much. But they were delicious."

"Thank you, honey."

"Now, time to clean this mess up. We have company coming."

Anna asked, "Who's coming?"

"We are having my friend Mike and Mom's friend Allison are coming over for the bar-b-que."

Tom started to clear the table and Karen stopped him.

"Tom, aren't you forgetting something?"

"What is it?"

"You're supposed to go out to the garage and get the hamburger and hot dogs out of the freezer."

"Oh, yeah. I'll be right back."

Tom went to get the meat out of the freezer. Then he came back to find that the table was clear, and the dishes were waiting for him.

"I didn't want you to feel like you weren't needed so I left the dishes for you."

"Thank you. Anything to feel needed."

Tom walked over and started to do the dishes.

"Why don't you go take your shower and I will clean up the kitchen?"

"That was the plan. Kids, go upstairs and get dressed."

"Okay, come on, Jeremy. Come on, Jake."

"Come on, Blue."

Tom finished up the dishes. He wiped down the counters and the dishes. Then he went in and settled down on the couch, turning on the TV to see if there was a game on yet. The kids came back down the stairs.

Anna asked, "Can we watch cartoons, Daddy?"

"Why don't you take your dogs outside and play with them out there?"

"Okay, come on, Jeremy. Let's take the puppies outside."

Karen walked back down the stairs to find Tom relaxing on the couch.

Karen asked, "Do I have to do everything?"

"What do you mean?"

"You could have the kids working on painting the planets for the solar system project."

"That is a good idea."

Tom got up and went to get the kids. He opened the door and called the kids over.

"Hey, why don't you come inside and get out your stuff for your project? You guys can start painting planets."

The kids came into the house and got out the Styrofoam balls and the paints.

"Please spread a newspaper over the table before you start to paint. I don't want paint all over my table."

"We will, Mommy."

They got out the balls, paint and brushes. They spread newspaper all over the kitchen table. Then they lined up the balls.

"Daddy how do I decide which color to use for which planet?"

"Well start with a charcoal color for Mercury. Do you know why?"

"Why?"

"Because Mercury is so close to the sun that it burns the surface and turns it like charcoal. Venus is yellow."

"Why?"

"Venus is yellow because of how the atmosphere reflects the light."

"What color is Earth?"

"Well, Earth is known as the blue planet. It is usually depicted as a blue planet with green land masses on it. Are you writing these colors down?"

"I am now. Let me catch up."

"Do you have it now?"

"Yes. What color is Mars?"

"Mars is known as the red planet. The surface is so thin that the color of the surface shows through."

"What about Jupiter?"

"Jupiter is multi-colored but the most interesting thing about Jupiter is the big red eye."

"What is the big red eye?"

"The big red eye is a storm that is several times larger than Earth and it has been going for hundreds of years."

"So, was it going on when you were a kid?"

"I'm not that old!"

"Really? Oh. Well, that is really cool."

"Yeah, that is cool. The colors are white, red, orange, and brown."

"What about Saturn?"

"Saturn is a yellowish brown due to its atmosphere. But the best part of Saturn is it has rings around it."

"Cool. What about Uranus?"

"Uranus is a green-blue color because of the methane in the atmosphere. It also has rings."

"What is methane?"

"Methane is a gas that can be produced by a decaying material or rotting material."

"The last planet, Neptune, what color is it?"

"Neptune is a bright blue and it has rings too."

"Thank you, Daddy, for going through all of that with me."

"It's not a problem. You know that when I was a kid Pluto was also a planet."

"Really? Why isn't it a planet anymore?"

"Well, they came up with new definitions of what is a full-size planet. Pluto is now called a dwarf planet."

"Wow, that is interesting."

"Now paint your planets. If you need help, then let me know."

"Okay, Daddy. Thank you."

Tom walked back into the living room and sat down on the couch.

Karen walked over and asked, "How are you doing?"

"Daddy told me what colors the planets are and why. It was really interesting."

"That's cool. Are you having fun painting?"

"Yes. Do you want to help?"

"Yes, I would love to help. Honey come back in here. Let's all paint as a family."

"Okay. I will be right there."

Tom turned off the TV again and walked back over into the dining room. They all sat down and started to paint.

Tom asked, "Which planet are you painting, Jeremy?"

"I'm painting Mercury."

"That's cool. What are you painting, Anna?"

"I'm painting the Earth."

Tom said, "I think that I will paint Jupiter."

They painted for about another hour and then it was time to get ready for their company to get there. Karen got up and walked into the kitchen.

Karen said, "Let's clean up the table. Leave the balls so that they can dry and newspaper so that they have something to dry on. Let's put the paint away and wash out the brushes."

"Okay. Come on, kids. Take your dogs outside again."

Jeremy said, "Okay, I will take the dogs out."

Anna replied, "I'll clean the brushes and put the paint away."

The kids finished picking up everything that they could and cleaned up. Then they took the dogs outside to play.

"Is there anything that I could do to help you sweetie?"

"Sure, you can help me with seasoning the hamburger."

"What do you need me to do?"

"Can you hand me the marjoram, coriander, parsley, and rosemary?"

"Is that all that you need?"

"I already have everything else that I need. Would you do me a favor and mix everything into the meat? You know how I hate to put my hands into raw meat."

"Yes, I will do anything for you."

"Aww, how sweet. Now mix the meat."

"Yes, ma'am."

"You know better than to ma'am me."

"Sorry. It felt like a ma'am moment."

"It's never a ma'am moment."

"Let me guess. Think florist."

"Good guess."

"Do you want me to make the hamburger patties too?"

"Yes please. Thank you."

Tom mixed the meat and started to make hamburger patties.

"How big do you want me to make the patties?"

"Big enough for the buns but remember they will shrink so make them a little bit bigger. But also, something else, if you put a dent into the center, we won't end up with meat balls instead of patties."

"That really works?"

"Yes, if it's done right."

"Okay, you got it."

Just then the doorbell rang. Karen walked over to the door and answered it. Allison was standing there. Allison stood about five feet six inches tall and had long red hair. She wore a white blouse with blue jeans and white tennis shoes.

"Hi, how are you?"

"I'm doing good."

"Please come in. He isn't here yet."

"You know that I'm not here just to meet Mike."

"I know, I just hope that you guys hit it off. Come in and I'll get you something to drink."

"That sounds good."

Allison walked into the house and followed Karen into the kitchen.

"What can I get you to drink?"

"I will take a beer if you have one."

"Here you go."

"The patties are good to go. Now we just have to wait for Mike to get here."

The doorbell rang again.

"I will get that."

Tom walked over to the door and opened it. Mike was standing in the doorway when the door opened.

"Hi, come on in."

"How's it going?"

"Fine. We are just about ready to start cooking."

"Good. I'm starving. Hey, I saw another car out there. I thought that this wasn't a set-up."

"I said that I didn't know. I lied. I just decided to stay out of it."

"I have half a mind to leave."

"Don't do that. I would never hear the end of it."

Just then Karen and Allison came walking around the corner.

"She is the one that Karen wanted to set me up with?"

"Yeah, why?"

"Forget everything that I just said. She can set me up anytime."

Tom laughed and said, "You and redheads, I swear."

"What can I say? I like what I like."

Karen said, "Allison, this is Mike. Mike, this is Allison."

Mike said, "Hi, how are you?"

"Hi, I'm doing good. How about you?"

"I'm good. So, what do you do for a living?"

"I do a before and after school program for elementary school students."

"How is it working with kids?"

Tom walked out to start the grill. Karen followed him outside.

Karen said, "It looks like they are hitting it off. Mike said something when we walked around the corner, what was it?"

"He fell for how she looks instantly. He loves redheads."

"If I had known that I would have introduced them sooner."

"Working with kids is like a dream for me," Allison said. "I want to finish my degree so that I can become a teacher."

"That's cool. How much longer do you have to go to finish your degree?"

"I need one more semester and then I need to get my teaching credential."

"That sounds like it is close."

"Yeah, so close that I can taste it. I heard that you're Tom's partner?"

"Yeah, I have worked with Tom for a couple of years now."

"So, what's it like being a homicide detective?"

"I can tell you this, there aren't two days ever the same."

"Are you working on a case now?"

"Yes, we are investigating a murder that happened last Sunday, but the body wasn't discovered until Tuesday."

"That's awful. What happened?"

"A twenty-one-year-old girl was stabbed to death in her home."

"Was it a home invasion?"

"No, it looks like she knew her killer."

"That's horrible."

Tom stated, "I think that the grill is ready to start cooking. Mike, why don't you grab a couple of beers and come out and give me a hand?"

"Sure, on my way out. I want to talk to you some more later."

Allison smiled at him as he walked away. She then turned and walked over to Karen.

Karen asked, "How is it going?"

"Great, he is wonderful and cute."

Out at the Grill, Tom and Mike were talking.

"What do you think of her?" Tom asked.

"She is great. We are really getting along. I am definitely going to ask her out sometime before the day is over. Wow!"

"What?"

"I can't get over how quiet those dogs are."

"I know they are a dream. It is good that you like Allison, except now Karen is going to have a big head when it comes to matchmaking."

Meanwhile, in the kitchen, the conversation continues about Mike.

"Do you think that he will ask me out sometime?"

"If the way that he keeps looking at you is any indication then yes I think that he will."

"I hope that you're right. I feel butterflies when he looks at me."

"The food is ready! Karen where do we want to eat the kitchen table is still covered from the project?"

Allison asked, "Why don't we eat outside? It's a nice day out."

Karen replied, "That's a good idea. It is nice and warm out today."

Tom carried over the hamburgers and hot dogs to the table. Karen and Allison carried out some potato salad and beans to the table. Mike brought out the plates and silverware.

Karen hollered, "Kids, come have dinner."

The kids came running out to the table with the puppies in tow. Everyone sat down at the table and began passing food around the table.

"Those puppies are so cute," Allison commented.

"I was opposed to the idea at first, but I thought that every kid should have a puppy. We were only supposed to get one but these two were the last ones and the kids didn't like the same one, so we caved in."

"Well, with how well behaved they are I think that you made a good decision. What are their names?"

"The black one is Anna's and she named him Jake and the white one named Blue because of his blue eyes and the fact that he has blue marled on his face and rump."

Tom said, "Wow, the seasoning on this meat is really good, sweetie."

"Thank you, it's the same seasoning that I usually use."

"So, what's it been like with two new dogs?" Mike asked. "I thought that you were just getting one."

"We were just going to get one but when we got there, there were two left and the kids each wanted the other dog so after some deliberation Karen decided that the kids needed to be happy."

"The kids couldn't be happier with the puppies. They are already trying to train them."

Mike asked, "How did they react when you told them they were getting a puppy?"

"We didn't tell them. We just told them that we were going for a ride in the country. Then we stopped by a ranch and while we were talking, we let the kids play with the puppies. They didn't know that they were getting one until we told them to put the dogs into the car."

Allison said, "I bet they were surprised."

"They were. We told them to put the dogs into the car and Anna said, 'really?' It was so cute."

"So, do you guys think that you know who your killer is?"

Mike said, "We have two suspects that are hiding something, but we don't know what."

"Could they be working together?"

Tom said, "I don't think so because one is the ex-boyfriend of the victim and the other is the victim's best friend."

"Besides, we don't think the best friend did anything. We just think that she is hiding something."

"What do you think that she is hiding?"

"I don't know."

Karen asked, "What makes you think that she is hiding something?"

"It's just her body language."

"What about the ex-boyfriend," Allison asked. "What do you think that he is hiding?"

Tom said, "Well, he gave us one alibi after it fell through and then he gave us another one. Now we are waiting on a warrant for that one to fall through."

"So, he could be the one that killed her."

"Yes, but the problem is that his mother is covering for him right now."

Karen asked, "Can you prove that she is covering?"

"It depends on what comes out of this warrant."

Mike said, "If this pans out, I think that we could have our killer."

"Do you have any evidence to show more than opportunity?" Allison asked.

"That's the thing. We don't have the CSI report back yet or the autopsy report. When we get those reports we might have some evidence, hopefully."

"When do you think that you will those reports back?"

Tom said, "I'm hoping on Monday. I called the medical examiner on Friday and they said tomorrow. I'm not sure on the CSI report."

"How long does it usually take to get back?"

Mike said, "Usually about a week and the victim was discovered last Tuesday."

"This is all fascinating, but I have homework to do and work in the morning. Thank you for dinner. This was fun. I need to get going."

Karen said, "Thank you for coming."

"I think that I should be going as well. Can I walk you out?"

"I would love that."

Mike and Allison stood up and walked toward the door. Mike walked Allison to her car, and they stopped to talk.

Mike said, "I really enjoyed meeting you today."

"I enjoyed meeting you too."

"I was wondering if I could take you out sometime. I know that you're busy during the week with work and school, so what about next Friday or Saturday night?"

"I would love to go out with you next Saturday night. Let me see your phone and I'll give you my number."

Mike handed her his cell phone and she put her number into his phone and called herself.

"Why did you call yourself?"

"Because now I have your number too."

"Okay, have a good night. Drive safe."

"You have a wonderful night and you drive safe."

Mike watched as Allison drove away. Then he walked over to his car and left. Inside, Tom and Karen started to clear the table.

Karen said, "I think that Mike and Allison hit it off."

"Yes, you were right about that match-up. Mike really liked her. I think that he is going to ask her out."

"I hope so. Allison said that she got butterflies in her stomach every time he looked at her."

"Well, he said that he was going to ask her out tonight."

There was a ring tone coming from the other room. Karen went to look at her phone.

"Who was that?"

"That was Allison sending me a text. She said that Mike asked her out at her car for next Saturday night and she said yes."

"Well, I would hope so. Did she seem excited?"

"I think that she is on cloud nine."

"That's good. Well, I think the kitchen is clean. Do you want to go relax in the living room?"

"We have to get the kids in here to finish Anna's project."

"Oh yeah. Are the planets dry?"

Karen checked to see if they were dry.

"Yes, they are dry."

"Okay, Anna, get the wires out and we will put this thing together."

Anna came in with the wires and string.

"How hard is this going to be to put together?"

"It shouldn't be that hard to do," Tom said. "Karen, could you get my wire cutters from the drawer in the kitchen?"

"I have them right here."

"Thank you. Now, I'm going to measure the wire and cut it. Then Karen, you twist the wires together. Anna, you can put the planets on it in order."

"That sounds like a plan."

Tom started to cut the wires and Karen started to put the wires together but couldn't figure out how.

"How do you suggest that I put these together?"

"Try getting a pair of pliers out of my tool box and twisting the wires together."

"Anna, please go to my tool box in the garage and get my good pliers out and bring them in here."

"Okay, I will be right back."

Anna went running off to get the pliers from the garage.

"Since you have an idea of how to put this together why don't you put it together and I will finish cutting the wire?"

"Okay, you talked me into it."

Karen started to cut the wire into the proper lengths.

"Oh, wow, I'm almost done."

"That's because I did most of it."

Anna came running back into the house holding the pliers.

"Is this what you wanted, Daddy?"

"Yes, that is exactly what I needed, thank you."

Tom started to twist the wires together and they started to line up.

"Can I put the planets on yet?"

"Not just yet. We need to put the last few wires on."

Tom twisted the last of the wires together.

"Okay, now you can put the planets on carefully."

Anna started to put the planets on the wires. When she got done, she reversed two planets.

Karen said, "Anna, you have Jupiter and Saturn reversed. Switch them and it will be right."

"Okay, Mommy, is this right?"

"Yes, that is right. Now run along and get into your pajamas and tell your brother to do the same. It's almost bedtime."

Tom said, "First get your brother and both of you take your dogs outside."

The kids took both Jake and Blue outside to the far end of the yard and then came in and went upstairs.

"Now get your pajamas on and brush your teeth. We will be up to check on you in a minute."

Karen walked over and sat down on the couch next to Tom.

Karen asked, "Is it weird that I need a break from the weekend?"

"I know what you mean. I am so tired. This weekend was packed, and we didn't take any time to relax."

"I guess we should go upstairs and put the kids to bed."

"Okay, let's get up there."

Tom and Karen walked up the stairs to Jeremy's bedroom to find him playing on his bed with Blue.

Karen said, "Come on, Jeremy, it's time for bed."

"Okay, Mommy."

Jeremy climbed under the blankets and waited for his hug goodnight. Karen kissed him on the forehead and gave him a hug.

"Goodnight, buddy, I love you."

"Goodnight, Mommy. I love you too."

Tom leaned down and kissed Jeremy on the forehead and hugged him.

"Goodnight, chief. I love you."

"Goodnight, Daddy. I love you too."

Tom and Karen left Jeremy's room turning off the light on their way out. They then walked over to and into Anna's room to find her playing with Jake on the floor.

Tom said, "Hey princess, it's time for bed."

"Can I stay up for another half an hour?"

"No, we agreed that the later bedtime was only for the weekend or non-school nights. We can talk about a later bedtime for the whole week another time. Okay?"

"Okay, Daddy. I will go to bed."

Anna then picked up Jake and put him on the bed.

"Now you stay there, Jake, okay?"

Anna then climbed into bed with Jake. She pulled the blankets up around her.

Karen walked over, bent down, and kissed her on the forehead and then gave her a hug.

"Goodnight, honey bear. I love you."

"Goodnight, Mommy. I love you too."

Tom leaned over and kissed her on the forehead and then gave her a hug goodnight.

"Goodnight, princess. I love you."

"Goodnight, Daddy. I love you too."

Tom and Karen walked over to the doorway and turned off the light. They then headed back downstairs to relax on the couch.

Tom asked, "Do you want to watch TV for a while?"

"That sounds good. I do want to go to bed once the kids have gone to sleep."

"I'm good with that. What do you want to watch?"

"As far as I'm concerned, we can watch one of your cop shows if you want."

"Your wish is my command."

Tom turned on one of his shows, 'LA Rookie,' and sat back to relax. Karen cuddled up next to him and fell asleep. Once the show was over, he woke up his wife to go to bed.

"Karen, Karen, it's time to go to bed."

"What?"

"It's time to go to bed."

"Do you know how messed up that is, to be woken up and told to go to bed?"

"I know but come on. Let's go."

"Okay, but I want to stop and check on the kids when we go by their rooms."

Tom and Karen checked the doors to make sure that they were locked and turned off all the lights. They then headed upstairs. They stopped by Anna's room first.

Karen said, "She looks so adorable. That dog really seems to love her."

"Yes, she is, and I think that dog was meant for her."

They walked over to Jeremy's room and found Blue practically sleeping on him.

"Isn't that cute," Tom asked. "I'm so glad that we got these dogs. They seem to be really good for the kids."

"I guess they are worth the trouble, so far anyway."

"Come on, let's go to bed too. I'm tired."

"Me too."

They walked into their room and shut the door. They started to change into their pajamas and Tom turned to Karen.

Tom said, "You know you're really looking good tonight."

"Not tonight. I'm too tired."

"Okay. I will settle for falling asleep in your arms."

"That's a deal."

They finished changing and climbed into bed and fell asleep in each other's arms.

MONDAY

The next morning Tom woke up alone in bed. He got up, took his shower, got dressed and went downstairs. When he got there, he found Karen finishing up breakfast.

"What's for breakfast?"

"I am making sausage, eggs and toast."

"Sounds good, I'm in."

They all sat down at the table to eat.

Tom asked, "Anna what do you have going on today?"

"I get my new spelling words today. Don't forget, Daddy, you said that you would help me this week with them."

"Do you want to go over them tonight?"

"No tonight I will have to write the definitions and use them in a sentence. So maybe help me go over them tomorrow night."

"Okay, it's a date then. What about you, Jeremy? What do you have going on?"

"I don't know what we will be learning this week."

Karen replied, "I know that whatever it is you will be great at it."

"Thank you, Mommy."

"So, sweetie, what do you have planned for today?"

"I have to drop off your dry cleaning from last week."

"Pesky clothes. We should all just go without them."

"You couldn't do that if you even wanted to try."

"I know. I guess you're just going to have to keep driving them over there. Sorry."

"I could let you do it."

"Please don't make me do that."

"You know that I wouldn't do that to you."

"Well, thank you. I need to get going. Have a good day, all. I love all of you very much."

Tom walked around the table and kissed each child on the forehead and then gave a little bit more of a kiss to Karen. Then he walked out to the car and drove to work. When Tom got into work, he found Mike already there.

"Good morning, Mike."

"Good morning, Tom."

"What do we have going for today?"

"We are supposed to be able to get the autopsy report this morning."

"Yeah, I'm going to give them a call in a couple of minutes."

A uniformed officer walked in. She was about five foot five and her brown hair was up in a bun. She handed Tom a manila envelope. Tom opened the envelope to find the CSU report inside.

"The report said that the victim's blood was the only blood found in the house," Tom said. "There was a bloody fingerprint on the knife, but it was too smeared to run through the system. There is a note from the crime lab saying that if they could get a print, they could match it. The blood trail ended right outside the door. There were no other hairs or prints left behind by the killer."

"Nothing else?"

"That's it. There isn't anything else."

"That isn't much to go on."

"If we can get a print from suspects, we can match it. That's something."

"I guess that will have to do."

Tom's phone rang, and he picked it up.

"Hello?"

"Hi, this is Doctor Johnson."

"Hi, Doctor Johnson. Do you have the report?"

"Yes, I have the report for you, but you will get it faster if you come down to the morgue yourself and get it."

"Okay, we'll be right down."

Mike asked, "What's up?"

"She wants us to come down to the morgue to get the report. She said that we will get it faster."

Tom and Mike head for the car.

Tom asked, "Do you think that we could go by that Starbucks again? That coffee ruined me for drinking the coffee at the station."

"Yeah, we can go by Starbucks. I really got you hooked, didn't I?"

"Yeah, I guess I am hooked. Speaking of hooked, I heard that you asked out Allison."

"How did you hear about that so fast?"

"Allison is one of Karen's best friends. If you think that they don't talk then you have some learning to do."

"How soon after we left did she call Karen?"

"I think that she texted as soon as she walked in the door."

"You're going to know every time that I screw up, aren't you?"

"Welcome to being in a relationship."

"What did I sign up for?"

"Are you sorry that you asked her out?"

"God no, she is great. She is smart, funny, hot. I couldn't ask for more."

"Yeah, she is a great person."

"Here we are, let's go get our coffee."

Mike pulled into the parking lot and parked. They walked in and it was a little crowded. They stood in line and gave their order when they got to the front of the line.

"What would you like, sir?"

"I would like a chai tea, please."

"What size?"

"Venti, please."

"Can I ask your name?"

"Mike."

"And for you?"

"I would like a mocha latte, please."

"What size?"

"Venti, please."

"Can I ask your name?"

"Tom."

"That will be $10.14."

Tom said, "Here is $12. Keep the change."

"Thank you, they will be right out."

"Okay, thank you."

Tom walked away to wait for his coffee.

"How do you drink those chai tea things?"

"They are good, I don't know how you drink those mocha lattes."

"I like the chocolate flavor."

"Mike, Mike. Venti chai tea for Mike."

"Right here, I'm right here."

Mike walked up and got his tea.

"Thank you."

"Tom, Tom. Venti mocha latte for Tom."

"I'm right here."

Tom walked over and got his coffee.

"Thank you."

Tom and Mike walked out of the store and went to the car.

Tom said, "I love this coffee."

"I guess we'll be going there more often?"

"Yes, I think so."

"Where do you think that I should take Allison for our first date?"

"I would take her to a nice restaurant and maybe some dancing."

"Dancing?"

"She would brag about that for a while."

"Brag about what exactly?"

"Brag that on your first date you took her dancing."

"I don't exactly dance."

"You do for one date. She will want to help you, which promotes touching, which is a good thing."

"In that case I guess I can do it. Now for the restaurant. Where should I take her, Italian?"

"No, everybody goes to Italian. Take her to a French restaurant."

"Does she like French food? Or should I ask her what she where she wants to go?"

"No, she will expect you to have a plan. If you go to a French restaurant you won't be like everyone else. You will be original."

Mike and Tom drove into the morgue. The morgue had a small parking lot with a loading dock area to bring bodies in and out of the building. There was just enough parking for the staff and a few extra spaces for when visitors come. The loading dock was just a small garage overhead door big enough to move gurneys through the door.

Mike asked, "What do you think that she found?"

"Hopefully something to help us catch the guy. Let's go in and see what she has."

Tom and Mike walked into the morgue. It wasn't an overall large building, but it was large enough. There was a reception area to greet anyone coming for official business. Behind the reception area was a hallway that led to some offices and at the end of the hallway was the room. The room is where they conduct autopsies and store the bodies waiting to be identified. There were two autopsy tables in the middle of the room. There were 16 refrigerated doors to store the bodies along one wall. On the autopsy tables there was a hose to wash off the bodies and clean up the mess from the autopsy. They were stainless steel and approximately eight feet long. They were equipped with a magnifying glass and a drain for draining the water when cleaning the bodies. When walking into the morgue, Tom and Mike found Dr. Johnson standing over Kathy's body, which was on one of the autopsy tables.

Tom said, "Hey, Dr. Johnson, how's it going?"

"It's going good. I think that I have some stuff that will help in your investigation."

"Good. We could use a direction to go in. We have a lot of theories but no conclusions. So, what do we have?"

"Well, when I did the tox screen there were no drugs or alcohol in her blood stream. There wasn't any sexual assault evidence on her body. She was stabbed nine times in the abdomen and one final stab wound in the chest. It appears that the first stab wound was into the small intestines, but the fatal blow was straight into the heart."

"Does it appear that this guy knows what he was doing?"

"No, it appears that it was a crime of passion. The other stab wounds didn't hit anything vital; they look like he was in a frenzied state just stabbing at her. In fact, if the last blow didn't hit her heart she probably would have survived. It appears from the stab wounds that you're dealing with a left-handed killer. Judging from the angle of the entry wounds, this person stands about five foot eleven to six foot two. He used the knife like a sword at first, thrusting into her body, but when he dealt the final blow, he turned the knife and stabbed overhand with anger. I feel that when he gave that final blow is when he decided that he was going to kill her."

Tom asked, "So the stabbing was a crime of opportunity but then he decided to kill her in the middle of it? Could the stab wounds to her abdomen be a cover for the wound to the heart? Like he knew what he was doing but was trying to cover it up."

"I think that the wound to her heart was the last blow. I think that he got lucky in hitting the heart because the first couple of stabs were hesitant, like he didn't want to stab her. He pulled back at first and then he started to stab the knife all the way in. The last stab to her heart was full force. By then he'd committed to killing her."

The phone rang, and Dr. Johnson answered it.

"Hello?"

"This is Stephanie. There is a Mr. and Mrs. Jefferson up front here. They said that they are here to identify the body of Kathy Jefferson."

"Can you escort them back here? I will prepare the body. Give me about five minutes."

"I will be bringing them back in about five minutes."

They hung up the phone.

"The Jeffersons are here. They are here to identify Kathy's body."

"I have a rapport with them." Tom asked, "Would like us to stick around?"

"Yes, that might be a good idea to have someone that they are familiar with here to talk to."

Dr. Johnson covered Kathy's body with a sheet so that her parents didn't have to see the trauma. Stephanie walked the Jeffersons to the autopsy room.

"Hello, I'm Dr. Johnson I believe that you already know Detective James and Detective Turner."

Paul said, "Yes we do. Hello again."

"What he meant to say is I'm Susan and this is Paul."

"Nice to meet you. I just wish that it was under better circumstances. Your daughter is over here."

"Is that her under the sheet?"

"Yes, I am going to lift the sheet from over her face and all you have to do is say that it is her and then when you're ready I will put the sheet back. Okay?"

"Okay."

"Are you ready?"

Susan and Paul looked at each other and nodded.

Susan said, "Okay, we are ready."

Dr. Johnson lifted the sheet and pulled it down to show her face. Susan started to cry and turned into Paul's chest. Paul also had tears in his eyes.

"Yes, that is our daughter, that is Kathy," Paul said.

"Please cover her back up. I can't look at her like that anymore."

Dr. Johnson covered up Kathy's body.

"Thank you."

Paul and Susan turned to Tom and Mike. Paul asked, "Do you have an update for us?"

Tom said, "Well, it looks like it's leaning toward the fact that she knew her killer."

"Based on what?"

"There wasn't any forced entry and it looked like a frenzied stabbing. Like a crime of passion. That points to someone that she knows. It wasn't a planned killing."

"You're sure? Because I don't know anyone that would do this."

Mike asked, "Not even her ex-boyfriend?"

"Why? What's wrong with her ex-boyfriend?"

"He has a rap sheet with possession cases."

"That's possession, not murder, not even assault."

"We were just thinking that if he got mad enough who knows what he is capable of?"

"Just please find the guy that did this no matter who it is."

"That is what we are planning to do," Tom replied. "I will do everything in my power to find who killed your daughter and bring him to justice."

Susan said, "Thank you for your dedication. Honey, please get me out of here."

Susan and Paul walked out.

Tom said, "I guess we have our marching orders."

"Yeah, I guess we had better get going."

"Thank you, Dr. Johnson. Please let us know if you come up with anything else."

"I will give you a call if I find anything else."

Tom and Mike walked out of the morgue and headed back to the station.

Mike said, "That was heartbreaking."

"Was that the first time that you were there for the body identification?"

"Yeah, have you been there for one before?"

"A long time ago and believe me, you never forget their faces when they see their loved ones laying there."

"I believe you. I don't think that I will be forgetting Susan Jefferson's face anytime soon."

"The only thing that you can do is work hard and do your best to bring their daughter's killer to justice."

"Well, believe me, I will now be working that much harder after seeing that. It makes the victim more human or something."

"You have to be careful because it's easy to become emotionally involved in the case."

"What's wrong with that?"

"Then you start to let emotions control your actions instead of letting your brain do it," Tom said. "It can be dangerous when you get clouded by emotion. That's when the wrong people go to jail instead of the guilty ones."

"We wouldn't want that. Do you buy Paul Jefferson saying that she wouldn't know anyone that would kill her?"

"I know that it was someone that she knows well enough to let in the house. I guess it could be a delivery person or something.

Maybe someone pretending to deliver something and that's why we didn't find a box or anything."

"It could have been someone that was pretending to check for a gas leak."

"We will just have to let the evidence show us who it was."

Tom and Mike drove into the station and parked.

Tom said, "I want to look into that warrant when we get in there."

"It should be back by now. I did get it in before I left on Friday."

Tom and Mike walked into the office to find a manila envelope sitting on Mike's desk. Mike walked over and opened the envelope.

"Hey, this is the warrant that we have been waiting for."

"Well, let's go. We can get something to eat on the way."

"You're hungry?"

"Aren't you?"

"Yes, but you're never hungry until we get to the restaurant."

Mike and Tom walked out of the station and out to the car. Mike asked, "So where do you want to go to lunch?"

"I was thinking about that place that specializes in burgers. You know, Champs Burgers."

"You really like hamburgers, don't you?"

"They are the best food."

"Okay. Where is this place?"

"It's not that far away. Just go up Main Street to Twenty-First and it will be just past that on the right."

"Okay, that is only a few miles away. So, what is so special about the burgers here?"

"These burgers are made with extras put on."

"Like what extras?"

"One has lamb on it."

"Instead of the patty?"

"No, in addition to."

"What else do they have?"

"They have all kinds of things like brisket, deep fried mozzarella cheese, mac and cheese and more."

Mike asked, "They put mac and cheese on a burger?"

"Yeah, I tried it. It's pretty good."

They pulled into the driveway of the restaurant and it was packed. It was a large parking lot of a strip mall. They had to park in the back because there wasn't any other place to park. The strip mall had a couple of different restaurants in it along with a department store and some small shops. Champs was located on the corner of the building. They walked in and the restaurant was crowded with one table available in the corner. Tom and Mike walked into the restaurant. There were booths along one wall and a set of two tables lined up in the middle with a wall between them. There were also two booths on the right side of the room. The chairs were a black metal with a red vinyl seat and the booths were a red vinyl seat and seat back.

"Are you sure that you want to eat here?" Mike asked. "It's awful crowded, it's going to take forever."

"No, it won't. They are pretty fast here."

"Okay, I will give it a shot."

The waiter came over to the table. The waiter was wearing a black and white striped shirt kind of like a referee shirt and black pants with white tennis shoes. He was also wearing a name tag that said 'Reggie' pinned to the left side of his shirt.

"How is everyone doing today? Can I get you something to drink?"

Tom said, "I would like an iced tea."

"We only have raspberry tea. Is that okay?"

"Yes, that will be fine."

"I will have a Coke."

"Okay. I will be back to take your order."

Reggie walked away.

"Raspberry tea? What does that taste like?"

"It's actually pretty good. It tastes like raspberries with a hint of tea."

Reggie walked back with their drinks.

"Do we know what we want?"

Tom said, "I'm ready."

"Yeah, me too."

"What will it be?"

Tom said, "I want to try the burger with the lamb."

"And for you, sir?"

"I would like to try the slopper."

"You both made great choices. I will have those out for you in a few minutes."

"Which one is the slopper?"

"It's served open face with chili and cheese on top of it."

"That sounds really good."

"I'm hoping that it is. Have you tried yours before?"

"No, I haven't tried this one yet. My fear is that lamb can be a fatty meat and I'm hoping that I don't get a mouthful of fat when I take a bite."

Mike said, "That would suck if that happened."

Reggie walked over to the table, bringing their burgers over with him.

"Here we go. You had the lamb and you had the slopper. Enjoy gentlemen."

Tom said, "Thank you. Wow, this looks good."

"Yes, it does. I think that I will dig in."

"How do you like it?"

"Okay. We can come back here whenever you want. How is yours?"

"This is pretty good. I would order it again. I just like to try everything."

"Oh, on that search warrant, I put in to get the surveillance footage as well," Mike said. "I figured that it would be helpful to be able to see how busy they were when he picked up his mother's medications."

"That was a good idea. I think that that will show a lot of information."

"There are holes in his alibi anyway. There is no way that he went to see his mother and then left right away. Then still didn't make it back to work for another hour."

Reggie came back to the table to check on them.

"How was everything?"

Tom replied, "It was very good."

"Can I get you anything else?"

"No, just the check please."

"Okay. I will be back in just one minute."

Reggie walked away.

Tom asked, "Whose turn is it to pay?"

"It's your turn. I paid on Friday."

"Are you sure?"

"Yes, you don't remember?"

"Yes, I was just giving you a hard time."

Reggie came back to the table with the check.

"You can take care of this when you're ready. I will be your cashier."

Tom read the check and it came to $30.74. Tom pulled out $40 and handed it to Reggie.

"I will get you your change."

"No change."

"Thank you very much."

"You're welcome. Let's get out of here."

"Okay, sounds good."

Tom and Mike left the restaurant and went to the car. They drove away and headed to the pharmacy to check John Murphy's alibi.

Mike asked, "What do you think that we will find out from this warrant?"

"I think that we are going to find out that he has been lying."

"Yeah but what has he been lying about?"

"That's the thing I don't know."

"I think that we are going to find out that he was there. I think that he is the one that killed her."

"You might be right, but we have to find the evidence first."

"Yeah, I hate that part."

"I'm hoping that the surveillance cameras caught something," Tom said. "How busy they were, the time that he got there and left, something."

They drove up to the Walgreens store and parked. They walked inside and to the back of the store to where the pharmacy was. Tom and Mike walked up to the counter and the pharmacy tech walked over to help them.

"Can I help you?"

"Yes, I'm Detective James, and this is Detective Turner."

Tasha turned around and said, "Detectives, you're back. I'll take care of them, Jenny."

"Okay." Jenny walked away.

Tom said, "Yes, we are back."

"Did you get your warrant?"

"Yes, here it is."

"Wow, this is my first warrant."

Mike replied, "Yes, well, any way can you get us the information that we need now?"

"Yes, what do you need?"

"We need to know when Sharon Murphy's prescription was picked up last Tuesday between 3 pm and 4:30 pm. We also need to see the surveillance recording from the same day during the same time."

"I can look up when the medications were picked up, but you will have to talk to management about the surveillance recordings."

Tom asked, "Can you reprint his receipt for us too?"

"If you say please."

"Please."

"I was just kidding but yes, I can reprint the receipt for you. This is just going to take a few minutes."

"Take your time. We will wait."

Tasha started to type on the computer for a few minutes.

"I think that I found it."

"Now can you print it?"

"Yes, it will take just a minute."

The printer started up.

"Here it is."

Tom looked at it and said, "Hey Mike, it says here that he got the prescription at 4:04pm."

"That means that he definitely wasn't at his house giving his mother the meds at 3:30 pm. Now we just need the security footage to see when he got here."

Tom asked, "Can you point us in the direction of the manager?"

"I can do one better."

Tasha got on the intercom and made a request.

"Ben to the pharmacy, please? Ben to the pharmacy?"

"Thank you."

"My pleasure."

Ben came walking back to the pharmacy area.

"Ben, these detectives need to speak with you."

"Hello, I'm Detective James, and this is Detective Turner."

"I'm Ben Walker the manager. What can I do for you?"

"We have a warrant to get the security footage of last Tuesday from 3 to 4:30 pm. Could you show us the footage and give us a copy of it? Please."

"Let's head back to my office and I can show you the video."

Ben led Tom and Mike to the back area of the store. They stepped through a door into a small office. It was about eight foot by nine foot. It contained one desk, one desk chair and two office chairs. There were a couple of bookcases on one wall and three filing cabinets on the other.

"Come on in and have a seat."

Ben walked around the desk sat down and started typing on the computer.

"Here is Tuesday's video file. Let me fast forward. Here we go. Here is the video starting at 3 pm."

Ben turned the screen to show to Detectives James and Turner.

Tom asked, "Can you fast forward to about 3:30 pm?"

Ben fast forwarded the recording.

Mike said, "I don't see him."

"Neither do I. Can you fast forward to about 3:40?"

Ben fast forwarded to 3:40. They watched for about 8 minutes and then found John walking into the store.

"There he is," Mike said. "Now let's see how long he is in the store."

"That's him leaving. He left at about 4:06 pm."

"That would give him time to get to his house and drop off the medications and then back to work by around 4:30 pm."

"But what was he doing from 3 to 3:48 pm?"

"I guess we will have to ask him that, won't we?"

Tom asked, "Can you make us a copy of this file?"

"Do you have a flash drive, or do you want me to put it on a disc for you?"

"I have a flash drive right here."

Tom handed Ben a flash drive to copy the file on to for them. Ben copied the file and handed it back to Tom.

Tom said, "Thank you for your time. If we need anything else, we will contact you again."

Tom and Mike left the Walgreens and headed for the car.

Mike asked, "Where to now?"

"Now we go pick up John Murphy again and question him about why he lied."

"I wonder what his alibi is going to be this time."

"I'm not sure. I'm hoping that we have him trapped this time and he admits to being there. Then we have a reason to get a warrant for his fingerprint. As soon as that comes back, we can possibility wrap this case up by tomorrow."

"That would be nice. Then we could get some closure for the Jeffersons."

"That would be a good thing."

"Where do you think he is?"

"How about if I call his work and see if he is working and just tell them not to say anything to him about us coming?"

"As long as he isn't the one that answers the phone."

"If he is then I will just hang up."

Tom dialed the phone number to 7-11. The phone started to ring, and a clerk answered the phone.

"Good afternoon thank you for calling 7-11. This is Rick. How may I help?"

"Don't say anything, I'm Detective James, do you remember me?"

"Yes, Det..."

"Stop. Don't say my name."

"Okay."

"Now just yes or no nothing else. Is John Murphy working today?"

"Yes."

"Okay. Thank you very much."

"You're welcome. Have a nice day, sir."

Tom then hung up the phone.

"Is he there?"

"Yes, he is, so we can head there."

"Yes, sir, we are on our way. Do you think that he will run when he knows that he is caught?"

"It depends on if he thinks that he can get out of it or not. Just to play it safe maybe I should go in the front door and you wait by the back door. In case he decides to run we will have him pinned in."

"That is a good idea. Why don't I ever get to be the one that goes through the front door?"

Tom said, "Because I don't know... Just do it."

"That's okay. I like going in the back door. Wait a minute, that came out wrong. I like to surprise the suspect when he is trying to run."

Laughing, he said, "Yeah, that sounds better. We can't talk to him until we get to the station so that he can sign the wavier of his rights. I don't want to mess this one up."

"Yeah that's a good idea. Okay, we are here."

"Park somewhere out of sight. We don't need him seeing us and running before we get into position."

"I will park in the back of the store."

Mike pulled the car behind the store.

"Okay. You wait here, and I will go around front."

Tom walked around to the front of the store. When Tom walked into the store, he found John Murphy stocking shelves.

"John Murphy, I have some questions for you."

John immediately ran toward the back door. The back door flew open and Mike immediately grabbed him and pushed him up against the wall. Tom came out right behind him.

"I didn't do it. I didn't do anything."

Mike responded, "Then why did you run?"

"Because I know that you will do everything that you can to pin it on me."

Mike frisked him and cuffed him. Then he put John into the back seat of the car. Tom got into the back seat next to him.

Tom replied, "If you didn't do anything then you have nothing to worry about."

"What do you want to ask me now?"

"We will get to that when we get back to the station."

"You guys are barking up the wrong tree. I didn't do anything."

Mike replied, "We'll see."

They drove the rest of the trip back to the station in silence. They drove up to the station and escorted John into the building and back to an interrogation room. Then they shut the door.

Tom said, "Sit down! I am now going to inform you of your rights. You have the right to remain silent. Anything that you say can and will be used against you in a court of law. You have the right to an attorney and to have one present during questioning. If you cannot afford an attorney, one will be appointed to you at no charge. Do you understand these rights as I have read them to you?"

"Yes, now can I get these cuffs off? They are hurting my wrists."

Mike said, "I will take them off but if you try anything they go back on. Now do you wish to talk to us about why we have brought you here?"

"Okay, okay. I won't try anything. Yes, I want to talk to you and clear my name."

"We checked your new alibi," Tom stated. "Your mom said that you were at the house dropping off her medication at 3:30 pm."

"See? It couldn't have been me. Wasn't she killed at around 3:30?"

"Yes, she was, but we went to the pharmacy."

"You did?"

Mike said, "Yeah we did, here is a copy of your receipt showing that you checked out at 4:04 pm."

Mike laid the copy on the table in front of him. John just sat there completely quiet.

Tom said, "That wasn't enough for us, so we went and got the security footage. It shows you getting there at 3:48 pm. And you leaving at 4:06 pm."

Mike asked, "What do you have to say now?"

"I didn't kill her!"

"Then what were you doing from 3 to 3:48?"

"I was taking care of a personal issue."

"Look, John, you have given us two alibis so far and neither of them have cleared you for this."

"All I can tell you is that I was taking care of ..."

"A personal issue. We get it. But do you get that we are investigating a murder and your word doesn't hold any weight?"

"You just have to trust me."

Tom asked, "You're a convicted criminal and you expect us to just take your word for it?"

"It's not like I have record for murder or even assault."

"It doesn't matter if you didn't have a record; we don't just take the word of a suspect. People tend to lie when they are guilty."

"But I'm not guilty so why would I lie?"

Mike asked, "How do we know that you're not guilty?"

"Because I'm telling you."

Tom said, "Get off it. It's not going to work. Now where were you from 3 to 3:45? We did have someone tell us that they saw a white truck outside of Kathy's house. Was that you?"

"Okay, yes, it was me. I drove by her house and I was trying to decide to go up to see if she was home. I wanted to talk her into taking me back and dumping whatever guy that she had taken up with."

Mike asked, "But you didn't go in?"

"I walked up but when I got to the door, I heard a scream and I thought that she was screaming because she saw me. The last time that I saw her she told me that she was going to get a restraining order against me. So, when I heard the scream I ran and drove away."

Tom said, "What a guy, you didn't even stop to see if she was okay."

"Like I said, I thought that she was screaming because of me. I didn't even know that she was hurt until you guys told me."

Mike said, "Well we have to hold you while we check your fingerprints. If it comes back negative, then you will be cleared, and we can let you go. Okay?"

"I guess that I don't have a choice, do I?"

Tom said, "No you don't. Come on, let's go."

John stood up and walked over to the door. Tom opened the door and walked him over to get his fingerprints. They took his finger prints.

"How long does it take to get prints back?"

"I expect that we will have them back by tomorrow."

"When they come back you will let me go?"

"When they come back, they will either tell us that we have the right guy or tell us to let you go."

"Well, I know that my prints weren't there, so I should be let go tomorrow."

"Yes, if you are telling the truth you should be home like a bad dream tomorrow."

"This is all a bad dream, Detective."

"You have a decision, you can either spend the night in holding or be processed because we are not going to let you go until your prints are back. If you choose to be processed, then you will have an arrest on your record. Which will it be?"

"Because I know that I'm innocent I would rather just stay in holding overnight."

"Come on. Let's go back to holding."

Tom escorted John back to holding and put him into a cell.

"Just sit tight here and we will get you out of here soon if you're innocent."

"Thank you, Detective."

Tom walked out to his desk.

Mike asked, "What do you think?"

"I don't know. He seemed calm when we told him that his prints could exonerate him or show that he was guilty."

"Yeah, you're right, he didn't seem worried at all."

"Well, I'm going to head out and see if I can get home at a decent time tonight."

"Yeah, I think that I'm going to head out as well. Goodnight, I'll see you tomorrow."

"Goodnight, I'll see you tomorrow."

Tom walked out and to his car. He drove home thinking if it wasn't John, then who could have possibly killed her? When he arrived home, he walked in and didn't find anyone.

Tom yelled, "Is there anyone here?"

All he heard was silence. Then he turned around to see headlights shine in the window. It was Karen and the kids coming home. They walked in carrying shopping bags.

"I'm sorry that we weren't home when you got here. I was going to call to let you know but I was so sure that we were going to make it home before you."

"It's okay, sweetie. I was just a little worried that's all. What did you get?"

"We stopped by Walmart and I got each of the kids a new shirt and myself some jeans plus a few food items that we were out of."

"That sounds good. What are we doing for dinner?"

"I thought ahead, and I bought Kentucky Fried Chicken."

"That sounds great. I love KFC!"

"I know, that is one of the reasons that I got it tonight."

"Okay, kids, let's get the table set."

The kids came in and started to set the table.

"Let's use paper plates tonight and cut down on the dishes."

Anna said, "Okay, Daddy."

They all sat down at the table to eat.

Tom asked, "Jeremy, what piece of chicken do you want?"

"I want a breast."

"Okay, here you go. Anna, what do you want?"

"I want a leg."

"Okay, here you go. So, how was everyone's day?"

"I got my new spelling words. Do you want to see them, Daddy?"

"After dinner, princess. How about you Jeremy?"

Jeremy said, "We are working on reading."

"Maybe after dinner when Anna is going over her spelling words with me you can do some reading with Mommy."

Karen responded, "I think that would be a good idea."

Tom asked, "Anna, are your words really hard this week?"

"Yes, they are really hard. They are compound words."

"Well, with your dad's help you will get them."

"Is all of your homework done?"

Anna said, "Yes. Mommy took us to the library today and I did it there."

"What about you, Jeremy?"

"Yes, I got mine done."

"Good. Hey, how did the solar system project go over?"

"I got an A on it. Thank you for your help."

"No problem. It was my pleasure to help."

"How was your day, honey?"

"My day was not a good day. We have someone in custody but with the way that he is acting I think that he might not be the one that we are after."

"What do you mean?"

"Well, his fingerprints will either exonerate him or tell us that he is guilty. He is acting like he just needs to wait for his prints to come back and he will be free. So, unless he planted some-one else's prints there, which I doubt, then he will be innocent."

"Do you have any other suspects?"

"Not any good ones. So, if this doesn't pan out then we are back to square one."

"That's not good. I hope something works out, if for nothing else than to give that family some closure. Is everyone done?"

Anna said, "Yes, Mommy."

"I will help you clear. We can all help clear. Right, kids?"

The kids in unison said, "Right!"

Everyone grabbed plates, containers, and silverware and took them to the kitchen. Tom washed up what little there was to wash, and Karen put the food away in the refrigerator.

Karen said, "Kids, take your dogs out before doing any-thing else."

"Okay Anna, why don't you go get your spelling words?"

"Okay, Daddy, I will go get them."

Anna ran over to her backpack and pulled out a sheet of pa-per. Then she walked back over to her dad in the living room.

"Here you go, Daddy."

"Okay, spell suntan."

"s-o-n-t-a-n. Is that right?"

"It's s-u-n-t-a-n. It's sun like sun in the sky."

"Oh, okay."

"Try notebook."

"n-o-t-e-b-o-k"

"It's n-o-t-e-b-o-o-k. There are two o's in notebook. Try something."

"s-o-m-t-h-i-n-g"

"Okay, that one is s-o-m-e-t-h-i-n-g. The e is silent. Why don't you go and study these and we can try again to tomorrow night before you go to bed? Okay? Don't worry, you will get this. You just need to study them a little and you will start to get them right. Okay?"

"Okay, Daddy. I will study them hard."

"Go ahead and go upstairs and get ready for bed but first get your brother and take the dogs outside. Then read through your words a couple of times don't try to spell them just read them at least three times. Then you can play before bed and we will be up in a little bit to tuck you guys in."

"Okay, Daddy."

Anna went up the stairs to her room just as Karen was coming back downstairs.

"How did the reading go?"

"The reading went good except that he gets bored with it fast. Other than that, he is a good reader."

"Then we need to get him more interested in reading."

"Why don't we do this? In the evenings after dinner you work with Anna on her spelling and I will go read with Jeremy. If he must do it every night, then maybe after time it won't be so boring."

"That's a good idea. You don't mind doing it?"

"Spending quality time with our son, not at all. I love to hang out with our kids."

"I was just thinking that you're with the kids all afternoon, it seems like you would want a break."

"Yeah sometimes I need a break, but I would really like it if he would learn to love reading instead of video games and movies."

"I don't think that we will keep him from loving video games and movies but maybe he could also love to read."

"That is the goal."

"I think that it's time to get the kids into bed."

"Back up the stairs. Sometimes I get tired of going up and down the stairs all day."

"I can understand that."

"Let's go."

Tom and Karen walked back up the stairs and into Jeremy's room. They found him falling asleep on his bed with a car in his hand. Blue was already in bed with him.

Karen said, "Come on, buddy, it's time to go to bed. Get under the covers."

"Okay, Mommy."

Karen leaned over him and kissed his forehead and gave him a hug.

"Goodnight buddy, I love you."

"Goodnight, Mommy, I love you too."

Tom walked over and bent down and kissed him on the forehead and gave him a hug.

"Goodnight, chief. I love you."

"Goodnight, Daddy. I love you too."

They left Jeremy's room and turned off the light as they left. They walked over to Anna's room to find her playing with Jake. She was training him to stay.

Karen said, "Honey bear, it's time for bed."

"Come on, Jake. Let's get into bed."

Anna picked Jake up and put him into the bed. Then she climbed in and pulled up the covers. Karen bent down and kissed her on the forehead and gave her a hug.

"Goodnight, honey bear. I love you."

"Goodnight, Mommy. I love you too."

Tom walked over and leaned over and kissed her on the forehead and gave her a hug.

"Goodnight, princess. I love you."

"Goodnight, Daddy. I love you too."

They walked out of Anna's room, turning off the light as they left. They walked back downstairs and settled onto the couch. They turned on the TV.

Tom asked, "What do you want to watch?"

"I don't care as long as it's only an hour long."

"Why do you only want to watch for an hour?"

"Because that should be long enough for the kids to fall asleep and I want to go to bed early tonight."

"Why? Are you tired?"

"No, I'm not tired."

"Oh, wait but why... Oh!"

"I know that you had a long day. Are you okay with that?"

"Yes, it will be the perfect end. Go to sleep, kids. Go to sleep."

"That's funny but I don't think it will work. So, what happened today that has had you so worked up?"

"We got the autopsy report, CSU report, and we were there for the body identification."

"I'm sure that was hard to see those parents in their worst moment of their lives."

"It was. I've only had to be there for the identification one other time before. This was Mike's first time."

"How did he handle it?"

"He handled it pretty well. But I'm sure that he's thinking about it now. I will ask him how he is doing tomorrow morning."

"That's a good idea. Do you think that the kids are asleep yet?"

"It's worth a shot to check."

"Okay, let's go."

Tom and Karen got up and walked up the stairs. They stopped by Jeremy's room and found him sound asleep with Blue laying across his stomach also sound asleep. Then they walked over to Anna's room to check on her. They found Anna sleeping with a doll in her arms and Jake was sleeping, snoring up next to her legs.

Karen said, "They are so cute, and those dogs have really taken to them."

"Yes, they are, and the dogs haven't been that much trouble so far."

"I think that we have your dog door to thank for that."

"And for making the dogs go out every few hours."

"Right, that too. Now let's go to bed."

"I like that idea."

"I thought that you would."

They walked into their room and shut the door. Karen kicked off her shoes.

"Are you sure you're up for this? You seem tired."

"I'm fine, believe me I'm up for this."

Tom walked over to Karen and kissed her passionately. Then he laid her back on the bed.

TUESDAY

The next morning Tom woke up by his alarm to find himself alone in bed. He took his shower and walked downstairs. Karen was in the kitchen making breakfast.

Tom asked, "What's for breakfast?"

"I'm making waffles."

"You only make waffles when you're in a really good mood."

"Well, I'm in a great mood. I had a really good night last night."

Tom walked over behind Karen and wrapped his arms around her and kissed her on the cheek.

"So, what happened last night that put you in such a good mood?"

"Well, this guy that I know just showed me a really great time."

"Just some guy? Huh?"

"Yeah, just a guy. You wouldn't know him. Kids, breakfast is ready."

Everyone sat down for breakfast.

"This looks good. Thank you, sweetie, for breakfast."

"You're welcome, honey."

Tom asked, "Anna, what is the homework tonight?"

"I have to write my spelling words five times each."

"That will really help you learn to spell the words and after dinner we will go over them again."

"Okay, Daddy, thank you."

"You're welcome. Jeremy, how's your reading going?"

"I think that it's going okay."

"Your mom thinks that you're a pretty good reader. Karen, what are your plans for the day?"

"Well, I was going to take the kids to school and then rush home and set up for a party. Then go wild at a party and clean up before the kids get home."

Anna said, "I want to go to a party!"

"Your mom is just kidding. Right?"

"Maybe. You will never know, will you?"

"Sometimes you scare me."

"Did you ever think that that is the point? Okay, kids, let's get your plates over to the sink. We need to go and get you to school."

The kids got up from the table and took their plates over to the sink.

Karen said, "Get your backpacks!"

"Princess don't forget your list of spelling words. You took them upstairs with you when you went to bed."

"Thank you, Daddy."

She ran up the stairs to her room to get her list. Then she came running back down the stairs with Jake following close behind. The kids ran over and gave Tom a hug goodbye.

"Have a good day I will see you tonight."

Karen walked over to Tom.

"It's my turn but I want a kiss."

Karen leaned down and kissed Tom and then pulled away, leaving him almost falling over.

"That's just teasing me."

"You know, always leave them wanting more."

"Who is them?"

"Wouldn't you like to know."

"You really do scare me sometimes. I love you!"

"I know; isn't it great? I love you too."

Tom left for work and Karen left with the kids to go to school. When Tom got to the office, he saw that Mike was already there.

"Good morning, Mike."

"Good morning, Tom."

"How are you doing after yesterday?"

"You were right. It does weigh on you."

"I told you, if you want to talk about it you can talk to me. I've been there and when I experienced it for the first time my partner did the same for me."

"Okay, I will keep that in mind."

"Did John Murphy's prints come back yet?"

"I haven't heard anything yet."

"Okay. I will call them and see what the holdup is."

Tom picked up his phone and started dialing. Just then an officer walked in and handed Tom a manila envelope. Tom hung up his phone and opened the envelope.

"Here is the report."

"The report about the prints?"

"Yeah, and you're not going to believe this."

"What is it?"

"John isn't our killer."

"I thought that he was way too calm. So, what do you want to do now?"

"Well, first things first. We have to go let John go."

"Do you want me to do it?"

"No, I'll take care of it."

Tom walked back to holding and looked at John.

"Well, did they come back?"

"Yes, they came back."

"Then I can go home?"

"Are you that confident that they didn't match?"

"Yes, I am."

"Yes, you can go. They didn't match."

Tom opened the cell door and motioned for him to leave.

"Come on, let's go get your personal effects."

Tom led John out to a side door.

"If you step through that door there is a window to your right. Give them your name, and they will give you your personal effects."

"Okay. Thank you, detective. Have a good day."

"You too."

Tom walked back to his desk where Mike was waiting.

"He didn't even ask if they matched. He just asked if they were back and when I said yes, he asked if he could go home."

"Was that it?"

"He also told me to have a nice day when he was leaving. It was weird."

"That is weird. So, what do we do now?"

"I'm thinking that we haven't gone to her school yet."

"You mean the community college?"

"Yeah, what do you think? Do you want to take a ride?"

"Sounds like fun. Let's go."

Tom and Mike walked out to the car and pulled out of the driveway.

Mike asked, "So what are we going to do when we get there?"

"I think that we will see about getting her class schedule and maybe go to one of her classes and interview some students."

"That's a good place to start."

"I thought so. We just need a new lead and I think that her friends from school will shine a light on some things. Besides, we still don't know what Kait Thompson is hiding."

"Do you think that she did it?"

"I don't know but she is still hiding something. I just want to know what that is."

Mike replied, "Yeah it would be nice to know what she is hiding. How is everything at home?"

"Fine. Why do you ask?"

"It's just that talking to you, things seem to have gotten to be routine."

"Yeah, I guess we do the same things every night. What do you suggest?"

"Have you thought about taking your wife out on a date night?"

"Do you think that she will have the energy to go? She seems to be tired all of the time."

"We are here. We will talk about this later."

"Okay. If you insist."

As they pulled into the parking lot, they found it full of cars. The building was a large, odd-shaped building. There appeared to be several buildings strung together by internal hallways. When they got to the college, they went to the Student Services Department. When they entered the building, it was busy. There were students walking everywhere of all ages. There was a long hallway with offices on the right side and then there was a long counter on the left side. The counter was where the Student Services Office was located. Tom and Mike walked up to the desk, cutting the line. There was a young woman sitting behind the counter. She had long blond hair with a French braid, thin and looked about twenty-five years old. When she stood up, she was about five foot five. She was wearing a blue blouse, black jeans, and white tennis shoes. She was also wearing a name tag that said Shannon.

Tom said, "Excuse me?"

"Sir, you need to wait in line like everyone else."

"Look, Shannon, is that your name? I'm a police detective. I need to talk to your dean of students."

"Oh, I'm sorry. I'll go get her right away."

"Thank you."

Shannon walked out of sight around a corner to the office of the dean of students. When she reappeared, she had the dean in tow. The dean was tall, about five foot ten, one hundred and eighty-five pounds. She had long brown hair, wearing a dress with a bright flower print and black low heels.

"Hello, I'm Dr. Lisa Taylor. I'm the dean of students here. How can I help you?"

"Hello, I'm Detective Turner and this is Detective James. We are here investigating the murder of one of your students."

"Oh my God, who was killed?" she responded in shock.

Tom replied, "Kathy Jefferson was killed a week ago Sunday afternoon sometime. We were wondering if we could get a copy of her schedule so that we could talk to her friends, classmates and teachers."

"Yes, I will look it up right away. Why don't you come back to my office?"

As they walked to the back behind the counter, the room opened into some cubicles with offices going around the outside of the room. The dean's office was in the back corner. When they walked in, they saw a desk to the left with a desk lamp sitting on it and a desk chair sitting behind it and two arm chairs sitting side by side in front of the desk. To the left was a couch with two chairs and a metal and glass coffee table in front of all three of them. There was a floor lamp behind the couch.

As they walked in, Lisa said, "Please have a seat."

Tom and Mike both sat down in the chairs facing the desk and Lisa sat down at the desk and immediately got on her computer. Lisa started typing and it brought up Kathy's schedule.

"Would you like me to print this up for you?"

Tom responded, "Yes, would you please? That would be very helpful."

Lisa typed on the computer for a couple of seconds and then the printer started up and the paper started to print. When it was done, Lisa reached up and grabbed the schedule and handed it to Tom.

"Here you go. I hope that it is helpful."

"Thank you, it will help us out a lot."

Tom and Mike headed out of the dean's office reading the schedule.

Tom stated, "Well, it looks like on Monday and Wednesday she was taking Math 121 from 10 to 11:50 am and English 121 from 2 to 3:15 pm and on Tuesday and Thursday she was taking Speech 115 from 10 to 11:15 am and Sociology 101 from 2:30 to 4:40 pm. Where do you want to start?"

"Well, the only class that is left today is her sociology class, so I guess that we should start there."

"The class starts in about three hours. So, let's go get some lunch and we will go from there."

Tom and Mike walked out of the college and back to the car. They then drove off to go to lunch.

"Where do you want to go to lunch?"

"I don't know. How about that Thai restaurant Thai Palace?"

"I don't think that we have ever been there."

"We haven't. I have always wanted to try Thai food, but I never did."

"Okay, I guess Thai food for lunch then."

"You don't mind, do you?"

"No, I don't mind."

"Are you sure?"

"I'm sure. I would tell you if I wasn't."

"Okay, thank you. I think that it is right up here."

When they pulled into the parking lot it was filled with cars. The building was sitting in the middle of the parking lot for a strip mall. It was a large building with a green tin roof and made of red brick with windows on all sides but the back. When they walked in, the walls in the dining room were lined with booths and there were tables filling up the middle. There was a red oriental lantern shining on every table. A hostess walked over to seat them. She was wearing a green button-up shirt with black pants and black tennis shoes.

"Is it just the two of you?"

Tom said, "Yes."

"Right this way."

The hostess led them to a table in the middle of the room.

The hostess said, "Tammy will be your server, she will be right with you."

"Okay, thank you."

Tammy walked over to the table. She was dressed in black pants and a red button-up shirt and wearing a black apron and black tennis shoes.

"Hi, my name is Tammy and I will be your server today. Can I get you anything to drink?"

Tom said, "I would like a glass of iced tea."

"I would like a Coke."

"Is Pepsi okay?"

"That will be fine."

"I will get those drinks for you while you look at the menu."

"Thank you."

Tammy walked away, and they looked at the menu.

"I don't know what I want to try," Tom said.

"I think that I'm going to try the Thai Red Curry with chicken, red peppers and bamboo shoots."

"That sounds good. I'm thinking that I'll try the same."

Tammy came back with their drinks.

"Are you ready to order?"

Mike replied, "Yes we are."

"What will it be?"

"We are going to try two of the Thai Red Curry with chicken, red peppers and bamboo shoots."

"That is a good choice."

Tom asked, "Is it really a good choice? Because neither of us have ever had Thai food."

"Yes, it is good. I've had it myself and I like it."

"Thank you."

Mike said, "Now back to your home life."

"What about my home life?"

"The fact that it is routine."

"What's wrong with routine? What about yours?"

"What about my life?"

"Well, when was the last time that you went out on a date?"

"Don't you remember? I have a date set for Saturday."

"Oh yeah. I forgot about that."

"Yeah, you were just trying to redirect the conversation away from you."

"I know, you're right. Sorry."

Tammy walked back over with their food. The air filled with the smell of curry and chicken.

"Here we go. Enjoy your lunch."

Tom replied, "Thank you."

"You're welcome."

"Now when was the last time that you took your wife out on a date?"

"I know, it has been a while."

"How long?"

"I think that the last time was at the beginning of March."

"That was a month ago."

"I know. It's been a while."

Tammy walked over and said, "Is there anything else that I can get you?"

Mike said, "Just the check, please."

"I have it right here."

Tammy laid the check folder on the table.

"I will be your cashier when you are ready."

Mike looked at the check and it was $35.60. He laid $45 in the folder.

"You had all kinds of advice when it came to me taking out Allison. Why don't you take your own advice?"

"That was for your first date."

"Why don't you try taking your wife back out on a first date? I'll bet that she would love it."

"You're probably right."

Tammy walked over and said, "I will bring back your change."

Mike said, "No change."

"Thank you. Have a nice day."

Tom and Mike left the restaurant and started back to the college. Tom said, "Well, I guess it's back to college for us."

"I always said that after the academy I wouldn't sit in another classroom again."

"Well, this time you aren't the student."

"True. I guess that will make a difference."

"It makes a difference for me. I have taught classes and believe me that is a lot more fun."

"Yeah, but we won't be teaching either."

"We get to talk to the class and interview students."

"Yeah, too much like work," Mike said.

"Well, we are back and now we have to try to find a parking spot."

"That is why they have these spots that are for police only."

"Why didn't we use this spot this morning?"

"Because I found a spot and I wasn't thinking about it. Where to now?"

"Let's go see this Edward Johnson and see if he will give us a chance to talk to the class and then we could talk to them individually. That way we can get to more of them," Tom said. "Otherwise, we are going to have to track all of them down separately and that will take a lot longer."

"Let's go see if Professor Johnson is in his office."

"Sounds like a good idea."

Tom and Mike started to navigate the college halls to find the faculty offices. The halls were wide with red and white walls and a polished tile floor. There were several areas off the main hallway for students to sit, study, and visit their friends and classmates. After walking for about twenty minutes they came to a door that said faculty offices. They walked through the door and found a desk sitting up front with a work study student sitting behind it. The work study student was wearing a red T-shirt with blue jeans and red tennis shoes. He was also wearing a name tag that said Mark on it.

"Can I help you?"

"Yes, I am Detective James, and this is Detective Turner and we need to speak to Edward Johnson. Is he in his office?"

"Let me check."

Mark picked up the phone and started to dial.

"Hello."

"Professor Johnson, there are two police detectives here that want to talk to you."

"I wonder what that is about. Can you walk them back here?"

"Yes, I will show them back."

"Thank you."

Mark hung up the phone and stood up.

"This way. I will show you to his office."

Mark started to walk them through a maze of cubicles and offices. There was a desk and chairs in each office. Once they made it through the maze of desks and offices they walked into his office. When they walked in it was a small office with a small desk and only two chairs in it including the desk chair.

"What can I do for you detectives?"

"Hello, I'm Detective James, and this is Detective Turner. We are investigating the murder of one of your students, Kathy Jefferson."

"What happened?"

"She was stabbed to death in her home on Sunday afternoon. We were wondering if we could come to your class today and talk to your students and interview some of them individually."

"Yeah, anything that I can do to help. You guys can have the first few minutes and then interview anyone that you need to at the back of the class."

"Thank you, this will be very helpful. Actually, could we ask you a few questions?"

"Yes, go ahead and ask whatever you need to."

Mike asked, "What do you remember about her?"

"Well, she was always in class, that is why it was so weird when she missed last week. Let's see she is, was a good student. She handed everything in on time."

"Did you ever notice anyone in particular that she would hang out with?"

"She hung out with a small group of people, one person all the time. I think that her name was Kait something."

Tom asked, "Was there a certain guy that you would see her around with?"

"No, not that I can remember. I heard her talking about an ex one time in class but that was it."

"What did she say about her ex when she was talking about him?"

"Well I heard her say that he was always there, and she thought that he was stalking her."

"Unfortunately, he has already been cleared, so we know that it wasn't him."

"Is there anything else that I could help with?"

"No, I think that is all that we have for now."

"Well, it's time to head for class anyway. Are you guys ready?"

"As ready as we will ever be. It's been a long time since I have been in a classroom."

Tom, Mike and Edward started navigating the halls at the school once again to get to the classroom. There were students everywhere. They went past several study spots and a café as well as the library. They finally came up on the classroom and Edward pulled out his keys and unlocked the door. As they walked in, several students filed in behind them and filled the seats. The classroom had rows of tables on either side with an isle down the middle. There were four chairs at each table facing the front of the classroom. There was a desk at the front on the classroom facing the tables. There were windows on two walls of the room.

When they got into the room they walked to the front. The students filed in just before the class started and started asking about who was in their class among themselves. The class was starting, and Edward walked up to the front of the class to introduce their visitors.

"Okay, settle down, we have some visitors today. These are police Detectives James and Turner. They want to introduce themselves and then interview a few of you one at a time at the back of the class."

Tom stepped forward. "As Professor Johnson said, I am Detective James and what we want to talk to you about is one of your classmates. Kathy Jefferson was murdered a week ago Sunday afternoon and we need to know everything that you know about her. How many of you were friends with Kathy?"

About six students raised their hands.

"Then you six, we will want to definitely talk to you."

A student raised his hand and asked, "What kinds of things do you need to know?"

"Things like if she is seeing anyone, is she fighting with anyone, does anyone like her that she has rejected, things like that."

Tom and Mike walked to the back of the room and turned a table so that they could use it to interview the students. They sat down, and the first student walked back and sat down.

Tom asked, "What is your name?"

"Samantha Reynolds."

"How do you know Kathy?"

"I have known her since high school. She was a good friend."

Mike asked, "I'm sure that she was. Do you know if she was seeing anyone?"

"I'm not sure if she was seeing anyone or not but I do know that she broke up with her boyfriend. I got the feeling that she broke up with him to go out with someone else."

"What gave you that idea?"

"I just know that after the breakup about a week later she got all happy and was humming to herself a lot."

Tom said, "Was there anyone that she was fighting with or was mad at her for something?"

"All I know is that she seemed scared of someone. She said that someone was creeping her out."

"Do you know who that person was?"

"I don't know, I'm sorry."

"Okay. Well, I think that will be all for now. Please give us your contact information so that we can contact you again if we need to."

Samantha got up and walked back to her seat. Another student walked over and sat down.

Tom asked, "What is your name?"

"Kian Walker."

"How did you know Kathy?"

"I met her here at the beginning of the semester."

Mike asked, "Were you involved with her?"

"No, but I would have liked to know her better. She was hot."

Tom asked, "Then what was the nature of your relationship with her?"

"We were assigned to be partners on a project at the beginning of the semester, that was all."

"Did she ever say that she was afraid of anyone?"

"Not that I know of. I'm sure there were other guys interested in her though."

Mike asked, "Do you know if she was seeing anyone?"

"Well when I met her, she had a boyfriend but then a month later she said that she broke up with him."

"Did she say how he took it?"

"All that I heard was that he didn't take it so well."

"How do you mean?"

"I heard that he was stalking her."

Tom asked, "Did she ever say any of this to you directly?"

"No, it's just what I heard."

"Okay, thank you for your time. Please leave your contact information so that we can contact you again if we need to."

Kian stood up and walked back to his seat and another student walked over and sat down.

Tom asked, "What is your name?"

"Chris Saddler."

"What was your relationship like with Kathy?"

"I have known Kathy ever since I started college last semester."

Mike asked, "Have you ever been involved with her?"

"No, I was with Kait for a while and then she broke up with me last month for no reason."

"Kait Thompson? Her best friend?"

"Yes, that is her."

"So, you know her from dating her best friend?"

"Yes, that is right."

"Did you ever have an interest in Kathy?" Tom asked. "She was an attractive woman."

"No, I was totally into Kait. I just didn't understand why she broke up with me. Things were going so well and then suddenly she broke it off."

"Well, back to the reason that we are here. Did you know of anyone that wanted to hurt Kathy?"

"No, but ever since Kait broke up with me I haven't seen much of her except in class."

"Do you know if she was seeing anyone?"

"I don't think so. I think that she broke up with her boyfriend about the same time that Kait broke up with me."

"Do you know if Kathy was afraid of anyone or fighting with anyone?"

"I don't know. I know that she always said that her boyfriend was a scary guy and she would hate to be on his bad side."

Mike said, "Okay, thank you for your time. Please leave your contact information so that we can contact you again if we need to."

Chris got up and went back to his seat, and another student got up and walked back to the table and sat down.

"What is your name?"

"Tina Andrews."

"How do you know Kathy?"

"I met her last semester, we had a class together."

"Do you know if she was seeing anybody?"

"I haven't seen her with anyone lately. It's just usually her and Kait hanging out. I hardly ever see anyone else with them lately."

Tom asked, "Have you heard of anyone stalking her?"

"I haven't heard of anything like that, but I did hear her saying that a guy was creeping her out."

"Do you know who?"

"I don't. I just remember her saying 'that guy really creeps me out' at the end of a conversation that I walked up on. I asked who it was, and she just said nobody."

Mike said, "Who was she talking to when she said that?"

"I don't know. She was on the phone. I think that she was talking to Kait."

"Did she have anyone that she was fighting with?"

"I don't know of anyone, I know that she and Kait have had some heated discussions, but I don't know what about."

"Do you know of anyone that was saying that they wanted to hurt her in any way?"

"I can't remember anyone saying anything like that."

Tom said, "Okay, thank you for your time. Please leave us your contact information in case we need to contact you again."

Tina stood up and walked back to her seat, and another student walked over and sat down.

"How does this work, do I just start talking?"

Tom said, "Let's start with your name."

"Okay. Jerry O'Brian."

Mike asked, "Well, Jerry, how do you know Kathy?"

"I know Kathy from last semester when we were dating."

"You dated the victim? Why did you break up?"

"Yes, we dated for a couple of months and then we decided to just be friends."

"So, in other words, she dumped you?"

"Yes, okay, she dumped me. She wanted me to be something that I wasn't."

Tom asked, "What did she want you to be?"

"In my opinion she wanted me to be a chick."

"What do you mean by that?"

"She wanted me to be emotional like she was. She wanted me to share my feelings and talk all night. She said that she wanted to be intimate, but she didn't want to be physical if you know what I mean. I don't even understand what she meant, and when I couldn't do what she wanted she broke it off with me. If she wanted to be with a girl, then be with a girl in my opinion."

Mike asked, "Then she moved on with that other guy?"

"Yeah, I didn't understand that either, because there was no way that guy was going to be what she wanted either. He was too much of a guy to be that way with her."

"Do you know of anyone else that she has moved on to now?"

"Not that I know of, but she has been overly happy lately and I don't know why. When she gets like this it seems someone new is there. We just don't know who it is yet."

Tom said, "Has she been fighting with anyone lately?"

"Not that I know of but, there have been some heated discussions with Kait."

"Do you know what about?" Mike asked.

"No, they seem to quit talking about whatever it is when someone else comes around and then they act all nice to each other again."

"Do you know of anyone stalking her?"

"No, I haven't heard anything. Why was someone stalking her? Is that who killed her?"

Tom stated, "We are just checking everything out. We don't know who killed her yet, but we will find out. Do you know anything that didn't seem normal about her lately?"

"Yes, she seemed like she was hiding something from everyone else. We just didn't know what."

Mike said, "Thank you for your time. Please leave your contact information so that we can contact you again if we need to."

Jerry stood up and walked back to his seat. The last student that raised their hand stood up and walked back to the table. Then she took a seat.

"What is your name?"

"Melissa Reese."

"How do you know Kathy Jefferson?"

"I met her through this class."

"What do you know about her?"

"I don't know much. I just started hanging out with her and Kait about a month ago. They seem to keep a lot of secrets."

"What secrets are you talking about?"

"Well, I don't know. I would walk up to them and then they were quiet and then changed the subject."

Tom asked, "Have you heard anything to give an idea of what they were talking about?"

"I think that they were talking about a guy. I think that they like the same guy or something because they said something like this could ruin their relationship."

"Are you sure that it was a guy?"

"I don't know, that's all I heard."

"Do you know which guy it was?"

"That's all I know about it."

"Do you know if anyone was having a fight with her?" Mike asked.

"I don't know of anyone else that she was fighting with."

Tom asked, "Do you know if she was having a problem with any ex-boyfriends or anything?"

"I know that she was talking about having trouble with her ex-boyfriend. He didn't seem to be able to take no for an answer."

"I think that we have everything that we need right now. Please leave your contact information so that we can contact you again if we need to. Thank you," Mike said.

"Mike, I think that we got everything that we are going to get."

"Yeah, I think that you're right. Let's go."

Tom stood up and got the professor's attention.

Tom said, "Thank you for everything. We will be going now. If anyone comes up with anything else, please contact us."

Tom and Mike walked out of the classroom.

Mike asked, "So what now?"

"Well, I'm going to go back to the station and then I'm going home."

"Okay, then what tomorrow?"

"I think that we should go back to the best friend, Kait Thompson, and see what she and Kathy were fighting about. Who the guy is."

"I agree."

They got into the car and started down the road to the station.

"So, if I plan this date night with Karen, who's going to babysit?"

"I see how this is going to go."

"What do you mean?"

"You're going to rope me into doing this for you because it was my idea."

"Hey, that's a great idea. How about Friday night?"

"How do you do that?"

"I don't know what you mean."

Mike said, "You made me offer to babysit for you."

"Awesome, try to be there at around 6, okay?"

"Okay, I will be there."

"I knew that I could count on you."

"Why did you pick Friday?"

"Because you're busy on Saturday."

"Well, that makes sense because you always planned on me babysitting."

"I plead the fifth."

They pulled back into the station, parked and then both left for home. Tom pulled into the driveway and looked through the window of the dining room. He saw Anna and Jeremy doing homework at the table and Karen cooking away in the kitchen. He felt an overwhelming feeling of love and pride for his family. He even had a tear in his eye thinking that in the blink of an eye it could all be gone. He got out of his car and walked into the house.

Tom yelled, "I'm home!"

Karen yelled back, "We are in the kitchen."

Tom walked into the kitchen and hugged each of his kids. Then he walked over to Karen and wrapped his arms around her and kissed her.

"What was that for?"

"Just because I love you."

"I love you too."

"What's for dinner?"

"There it is! We are having grilled chicken sandwiches with French fries."

"What do you mean there it is? You fired up the grill?"

"You always ask what's for dinner when you walk in the house," Karen said. "Yes, that one right there."

"Oh, the George Foreman Grill."

"Yes, it was easier."

"Are you kids almost done with your homework?"

Anna said, "Yes I'm almost done."

"Keep those spelling words out so that we can go over them later. Jeremy, what about you?"

"I am all done."

Karen said, "Except for reading to me later."

"Yeah."

Karen announced, "Dinner is ready. Honey, will you help me put food on the table?"

Tom walked over and helped Karen bring over the chicken breasts and the fries. Karen brought over the buns and the condiments. They all sat down at the table to eat.

"What gave you the idea to have this for dinner?"

"Why, do you not like it?"

"No, on the contrary, I'm looking forward to this. It sounds really good."

"Well, it was easy, so I figured that I would take an easy night for dinner."

"That is good. You cook almost every night, plus every morning and you fix the kids' lunches. You deserve to have an easy night cooking."

"Thank you, honey. I appreciate you saying that."

"Well, it's the truth. I love you."

"I love you too."

"Anna, do you think after writing your spelling words five times you have an idea of how to spell them?"

"Yes, Daddy, I think that I can do better tonight."

"Good, then we will go over them after we clean up from dinner. We are going to do everything that we can to get you an A on that test this week."

"Thank you, Daddy."

"You're welcome, princess."

Karen asked, "Jeremy, how did your reading go today in school?"

"I think that I'm doing okay. When I get done with my turn the teacher always says that I did a good job."

"That's great, Jeremy, I'm proud of you. Karen, this was a delicious dinner. I really enjoyed it."

"Thank you. It makes me happy that you enjoyed it."

"We should get this cleaned up. Kids, take your plates over to the sink and I will do the dishes if you clear, sweetie."

"That sounds good. Kids, once you put your plates in the sink take your dogs outside."

Anna said, "Okay, Mommy."

The kids got up and took their plates over to the sink. Anna helped Jeremy with his plate.

"The only complaint that I have is I don't like to clean that grill."

"You will be fine."

Tom and Karen got up and Tom started doing the dishes. Karen started to clear the table. The kids came back into the house from the back yard.

"The dogs are outside," said Anna.

Karen replied, "Thank you, honey bear, why don't you guys go get your pajamas on?"

Tom said, "Then get out your spelling words and go over them. Get ready for me to quiz you."

"Okay, Daddy I will."

"How is she doing with her spelling?"

"We'll see how she does tonight but last night I gave her three of her spelling words and she got all three wrong. I'm hoping that after studying last night and writing them out today, she will do better."

"I hope that you can get her to an A on her next test. She is hoping for it. Earlier today she was saying that she knows that you will help her get it."

"Well, I'm going to work with her as much as I need to get her there. That clean-up was easy."

"What are you going to do now?"

"I'm going to go and run through those spelling words with Anna. Are you going to go read with Jeremy?"

"Yeah, I'm headed up there right now."

"Anna, come down here with your spelling list."

Anna came running down the stairs.

"I'm here, Daddy."

"Okay, Anna, let me see the list. Try to spell inside."

"i-n-s-i-d-e. Is that right?"

"Yes, you got it right. Okay, give without a try."

"w-i-t-h-o-u-t. How was that, Daddy?"

"Very good. Can you spell ladybug?"

"l-a-d-y-b-u-g. Did I get it?"

"You're doing great."

Tom and Anna went over seven more words and she only missed two.

"Okay, princess, we went through half of them tonight and you got most of them right. So, study the two that you missed, and we will go over the other half and the two that you missed tomorrow."

"Okay, Daddy. Thank you for going over them with me."

Anna went running upstairs, passing Karen on her way down.

"Honey bear, it's time for bed. Your dad and I will be up in a few minutes to tuck you in."

"Okay, Mommy."

Karen came around the corner to find Tom sitting in his chair falling asleep.

Karen said sternly, "Tom!"

"What?"

"Come on, we need to go tuck in the kids."

Tom and Karen walked up the stairs and went into Jeremy's room to find him playing with his cars.

"Jeremy, didn't I tell you to get into bed?"

"I'm sorry, Mommy."

Jeremy picked up Blue and put him into bed and then climbed into bed himself.

Karen leaned down and kissed him on the forehead and gave him a hug.

"Goodnight, buddy. I love you."

"Goodnight, Mommy. I love you too."

Tom leaned in and gave him a kiss on his forehead and gave him a hug.

"Goodnight, chief. I love you."

"Goodnight, Daddy. I love you too."

Tom and Karen walked out of the room and turned off the light on their way. They then walked over to Anna's room to find her lying in bed with Jake by her side waiting on them.

"Princess, are you waiting on us?"

"Yes, I am, Daddy."

Tom leaned down and kissed her on the forehead and hugged her.

"Goodnight, princess. I love you."

"Goodnight, Daddy. I love you too."

Karen bent down and kissed her on the forehead and hugged her.

"Goodnight, Mommy. I love you."

"Goodnight, honey bear. I love you too."

Karen and Tom walked out of the room, turning off the light on the way. They then walked back down the stairs and collapsed into the couch.

Karen asked, "What were we thinking when we decided to have kids?"

"We were thinking that we were happy, and we wanted to share it. Nobody told us how much work it was going to be."

"What do you mean 'were happy'? Are you not happy?"

"That isn't what I meant. I am very happy. I just think that we need a break."

"No, you need a break."

"No, I mean we need a break together. I was thinking that I need to take you out on a date. Just the two of us. A real night out, not just dinner. I'm talking getting really dressed up, a nice dinner, and dancing."

"I don't know what to say."

"Say yes."

"Who would watch the kids?"

"I already have that arranged."

"Who did you rope into this?"

"Actually, Mike volunteered."

"That doesn't sound right."

"Okay, okay, I guess I kind of tricked him into it."

"That sounds more plausible. Is he really okay with this?"

"Yes, he knew what I was doing."

"In that case I say yes."

"That's great, I was thinking Friday night," Tom said excitedly.

"That sounds perfect."

"Now that we that settled that, do you want to watch TV?"

"Sure, what do you want to watch?"

"I was thinking one of my cop shows if you don't mind."

"They're not all that bad. Sure, we can watch one."

They watched TV for about two hours.

Karen said, "I think that I'm going to go to bed. I'm tired."

"Me too. I will be right behind you. I just want to check the door locks and turn off the lights."

"Okay, I will see you there."

She smiled toward Tom as she got up and headed up the stairs. Tom checked the door locks and turned off the lights, then followed her up. When they got upstairs, they changed and went to bed. They fell asleep pondering their coming date in a few days.

WEDNESDAY

The next morning Tom woke up and showered and headed downstairs. He walked into the kitchen where Karen was preparing breakfast for the kids.

"What's for breakfast?"

"We are having oatmeal with bananas in it."

"That is different, and it sounds good. Is there enough for me?"

"No, I would never make enough for you. Just kidding. There is just enough. Have a seat."

Tom took his seat at the table.

Tom asked, "So is it good, kids?"

Jeremy said, "It's really good."

"I really like it. I didn't think that I would, but I do."

Karen got herself a bowl and sat down with everyone.

"So where did this idea come from?"

"We are running late so I was looking for something fast."

"Why are you running late?"

"Because your arms are too comfortable."

"What? What do you mean by that?"

"Well, I was lying there with your arms still around me and I fell back asleep."

"And somehow that's my fault?"

"Of course, it's your fault. Whose fault should it be? Certainly not mine."

"I don't believe that it's my fault. I think that it's more your fault for falling back asleep."

"No, that can't be. Okay, kids, we have to go."

Tom finished and stood up, hugged his kids and gave Karen a kiss goodbye.

"I need to get to work."

Tom drove to work thinking that they should get over to Kait Thompson's house before she left for the day. Tom was the first one to the office. He was sitting at his desk looking through his notes from their last interview with Kait Thompson when Mike walked in.

"Good morning, Tom."

"Good morning, Mike. Are you ready to get going?"

"Where are we going again?"

"We have to go to talk to Kait Thompson."

"Oh yeah, you want to go over there this early?"

"Yeah, I want to get there before she leaves for the day. I also want to bring her in and put her in the box. Let's see her lie to us there."

"Okay, let's go get her."

Tom grabbed his jacket and they walked out to the car and drove out of the parking lot.

Tom said, "I'm tired of her just jerking us around like this. It's starting to make me feel like she is the one that killed her."

"Yeah, she has been hiding something all this time. If she wanted us to find her friend's killer, then you would think that she would tell us everything."

"Yeah, you would think."

"Unless she is involved."

"I still have trouble believing that she could kill her best friend."

"Yeah, but love will make you do things that you never would have before."

"What do you mean?"

"Well, if they were in love with the same guy then Kait might have killed off the competition."

"Yeah, that makes sense."

"She could have climbed out of her window and gone over to confront her and then it got out of hand. She ended up on arguing with her then stabbing her and when she saw what she did she decided that she had to kill her, so she stabbed her in the heart."

"That actually sounds plausible."

"You sound surprised."

"Maybe a little. You're not known for your plausible theories."

"True. We are here."

Tom and Mike walked up to the door and rang the doorbell. The door opened, and Richard Thompson was standing there.

"What do you need now, Detectives?"

Tom said, "We need to talk to your daughter."

"Kait, get down here. The detectives need to talk to you again."

Kait came down the stairs still in her robe.

"What do you need, Dad?"

"These detectives are back to ask you some more questions."

"What can I help you with, Detectives?"

Tom said, "You can get dressed and come down to the station with us."

"I don't think so, she isn't going anywhere with you."

"If she doesn't come willingly then we will arrest her, and she will have that on her record, or she can avoid that by coming willingly."

"Fine," Richard stated, "but it needs to be later because I have to go to work."

Mike said, "Go to work. We don't need to talk to you."

"I don't want you talking to her without me."

Tom replied, "You're not going to be in the room when we are questioning her."

"Oh yes I am. She is my daughter and I won't allow it."

"She is over 18 and we can question her without you."

"Then she is getting a lawyer."

"That is fine; she has that right. Have the attorney meet us at the station."

Richard walked away and got on the phone. Kait went upstairs and got dressed. Then she came back down.

"I'm ready."

"Your dad is having a lawyer meet us there."

"Dad, I don't need a lawyer."

"You are having a lawyer there. I'm not going to let them pin this on you."

"Okay, let's go."

Tom and Mike escorted Kait out to the car. They put her in the back seat and Tom got in the back seat on the other side.

"What do you need from me?"

Tom said, "We will discuss that when we get back to the station."

"You can't tell me something. Where are you at in the case?"

"We will talk about it when we get there."

"So, I'm supposed to just sit here and ride in silence?"

"That's kind of the idea."

"Fine, then I will just be quiet."

They rode the rest of the way to the station in silence. When they got there, they escorted Kait in the back door and into an interrogation room. They left her there alone for about ten minutes to observe her behavior. She sat down at the table and acted nervous. When her lawyer got there, he walked in and introduced himself to Detective James.

"Hi, I'm Ryan Clark. I will be representing Kait Thompson."

Tom said, "Yes, she is right this way."

Tom escorted him to the interrogation room.

"I will need a minute with my client."

"Okay. Let us know when you are ready for us to come in."

Mike walked over and asked, "Who is that guy?"

"He would be Kait's lawyer. They are conferring right now to get their story straight."

"I hate lawyers. They always get in the way."

"Yes, they do."

Ryan came out of the interrogation room.

"We are ready for you."

Tom said, "Come on, let's go."

"I love when they give us permission to come in."

They walked into the room and sat down.

Mike said, "I'm going to inform you of your rights. You have the right to remain silent. Anything that you say can and will be used against you in a court of law. You have the right to an attorney and to have an attorney present during questioning which you are exercising. If you can't afford an attorney, then one will be provided to you. Do you understand these rights that I have read to you?"

"Yes, I do."

Tom asked, "Okay, then, is there anything else that you want to tell us that you haven't?"

"I don't know what you're getting at."

Mike asked, "How about who did you break up with your boyfriend for?"

"There wasn't anybody."

"Who was the guy that Kathy broke up with her boyfriend for?"

"There was no guy. Besides, I have an alibi."

Tom replied, "There is a tree outside of your window that would allow for you to climb down and sneak out."

"But I didn't."

"You have no proof that my client did anything."

"Kait, we know that you were fighting with Kathy about a guy."

"Don't say anything."

"No, I'm going to say something. There is no guy!"

"Kait, we know that you were fighting with her about something that would ruin your relationship with her."

"Yeah, my relationship with her!"

"What else would possibly cause a problem with your relationship?"

"We both broke up with our boyfriends for each other."

Mike asked, "What do you mean for each other?"

"We were a couple," Kait said while tears were streaming down her face. "I would never hurt her. I was in love with her!"

"Oh, then why were you arguing?"

"We were trying to decide if we wanted to come out as a couple or not. That is what was going to ruin our relationship."

Tom said, "Okay, that makes sense. Is there anybody else that she was having problems with?"

"What about her ex-boyfriend, John?"

"We cleared him. Who else was she having problems with?"

"She always said that her neighbor creeped her out. But he is harmless."

"Which neighbor?"

"The one right next door to her."

Mike asked, "What did he do that creeped her out?"

"Well, he would always look at her when she was out front. She said the way that he would say hi and ask about her day seemed to be just a little too interested."

"Was there anything else?"

"Yes, her bedroom overlooked the street and she said that she caught him watching her from his front yard as she was holding clothes up to herself to see what they would look like on. That one really creeped her out."

"Did she tell anyone else about this?"

"No, she was too embarrassed to. She figured that she did something that would make him feel like that was okay. I told her that it wasn't her that it was him, but she still felt that it was her fault."

"You were right; that wasn't her fault."

"Can I go now?"

Tom said, "Yes, you can go."

Kait and her lawyer got up and walked out.

Tom turned to Mike and said, "I think that we should go talk to that neighbor again."

"I think that is a good idea. Maybe we can stop for lunch on the way?"

"Of course. You can't miss a meal, can you?"

"No, I can't. I would waste away!"

"You're not going to waste away, believe me."

"What is that supposed to mean?"

"Nothing. I was just kidding. Okay, let's get going. We will have lunch and then go to talk to that neighbor."

They walked out and went to lunch.

Tom asked, "Where do you want to go to lunch at?"

"I was thinking pizza."

"That really sounds good."

"Doesn't it? What do you think about this neighbor?"

"I think that this neighbor looks like a good suspect."

"After we talked to him at first, I didn't think much about him. He did seem harmless."

"I didn't think that he could be involved either, especially after it turned out that John was there, so he was honest about the white truck being there."

"Well, now he is our best lead."

"That is true."

"We are here."

"Gino's Pizza, huh?"

"Yeah, it's the best pizza in town."

"We'll see about that."

Tom and Mike drove into the parking lot. It was a medium-sized building with just a few cars in the lot. They walked into the restaurant and there were several tables in the middle of the room. The tables were metal with metal chairs and black vinyl seats. There were black booths lining the walls. A waitress walked over wearing blue jeans and a bright red shirt with a black apron.

"Just sit wherever you like."

Tom said, "Thank you."

They walked over and sat down at a booth.

Tom said, "I thought that red was a standard color for a pizzeria."

"Just wait until you taste it."

The waitress walked over, pulling out a pad of paper to take their order.

"Hi, my name is Joanne. I will be your server today. Can I get your something to drink?"

Mike said, "Yes, I will have a Coke."

"And I will have an iced tea."

"Great, I will be back in a few minutes to take your order."

Mike asked, "What do you want?"

"I usually like a supreme pizza"

"Me too, do you want to just split a medium pizza?"

"I think that we could make that work."

Joanna came back with the drinks.

"Do you know what you want?"

Mike said, "Yes, we are going to share a medium supreme pizza."

"What kind of crust do you want?"

Mike looked at Tom and said, "Hand tossed?"

Tom nodded his head yes.

Mike said, "Hand tossed."

"Okay, that will be out in about ten minutes."

Tom responded, "Wow, that is quick."

"Well, we aren't very busy right now."

"Thank you."

Joanne walked away to put the order in.

"So, I need to make sure that you're really okay to babysit this Friday."

"I wouldn't have said yes if I didn't want to do it. You guys are my best friends and I would do anything to help you."

"You are my best friend too, outside of Karen, of course."

"Of course."

"I think that's why Karen keeps trying to set you up. She just wants you to be happy."

"Don't worry. The kids and I will have fun on Friday. I was going to order pizza for them and watch movies maybe play games. It's going to be fine so don't worry about it so much."

"Okay, I won't worry about it. Thank you."

"No problem."

Joanne walked back over carrying the pizza. She set it down in the middle of the table on the stand. She also brought two plates and gave one to each of them.

"Here you go. I hope that you enjoy your pizza."

"Okay, let me try the best pizza in town."

"You're not going to regret this."

Tom and Mike each took a piece of pizza. Tom took a bite of pizza and just about burned his mouth.

"Wow, that is hot."

"It just came out of the oven. Of course, it's hot. But how does it taste?"

"You're right, it's really good."

"I told you."

"Okay, okay, you were right. Just don't get used to it."

"What do you really think? Do you think that this guy is our guy?"

"It's very possible."

"But what do you think?"

"Yes, I think that this could be him."

They finished eating and motioned the waitress over. Joanne walked over to find out what they needed."

"What could I do for you?"

Tom said, "We just need the check, thank you."

"I will be right back with the check."

"Are you in a hurry?"

"I'm trying to get over to get that guy, what's his name?"

Mike looked through his notes.

"His name is Todd Walker."

Joanne walked back with the check and placed it on the table.

"Just take care of this when you are ready. I will be your cashier."

Tom looked at the check and it said $19.36.

"Wow I got off easy this time."

"Why? How much is it?"

"I got away with under $20."

"I'll make sure that it is more next time."

"Thanks, I'm sure that you will."

Tom motioned for the waitress to come over again.

"Here you go."

Tom handed her $28 and said, "No change."

"Thank you, have a nice day."

Mike said, "You too. Now let's go pick Todd up."

Tom and Mike walked out to the car and drove down the road.

"That was a good lunch. Thank you for taking us there."

"No problem. I hate to arrest someone on an empty stomach."

"So, are you looking forward to your date with Allison?"

"Yes I am."

"Are you nervous? You sound nervous."

"Okay, maybe a little."

"Why are you nervous? It's not like dating is new to you."

"I know, but I really like her, so I don't want to mess this up."

"Don't worry. From what I gathered from Karen she is nervous too."

"She is? Why?"

"I think that she really likes you too."

"Well, that is good to know."

"Does that make you feel better?"

"Yes, a little. We are here."

Tom and Mike walked up to the door to Todd Walker's house. They knocked on the door and Todd answered it.

"What can I do for you, Detectives?"

Tom said, "You can come with us. We have some questions for you."

"Why can't you ask me here?"

"We just prefer to ask them down at the station."

"Okay, I guess."

They escorted Todd back to the car and put him in the back seat. Tom got in the back seat of the other side of the car. They drove back to the station.

"So, what sorts of questions do you have for me?"

"They are pretty standard questions. I wouldn't worry about it."

"Okay. I was just wondering. I just don't know why you can't ask me the questions at my house like you did before."

"We just want to make sure that your rights are not violated. That's all."

"I guess it's good that you're trying to protect me."

"Yeah, that is all that we are doing."

"Well, in that case, thank you for looking out for me."

"No problem."

They rode the rest of the way to the station in silence. When they got back to the station, they escorted Todd into the back door. They took him through the maze of desks and chairs to the interrogation room. Mike put Todd into the room and left him alone.

"We will be back in a minute."

Mike shut the door and walked over to observe him in the room.

Mike commented. "That's the first time that I have ever seen that."

"What did he do?"

"When we were in the car and he said thank you for bringing him in."

"Yeah, that is new. I don't think that I have ever had that happen before either."

Todd was sitting tapping his foot and then walking back and forth, then sitting again and tapping his foot.

"What do you think?" Mike asked. "Has it been enough time?"

"Yeah, I think that I've seen enough. He is nervous. Let's take a glass of water in to him to relax him and get his print."

"That's a good idea. I'll go get it."

Tom and Mike walked into the room to find Todd pacing. Mike placed a glass of water on the table.

Tom said, "Have a seat. We thought that you could use a glass of water."

Todd walked over to the table and sat down again, tapping his foot. Todd grabbed the glass and took a drink.

"You have the right to be silent. Anything that you say can and will be used against you in a court of law. You have the right to an attorney and to have one present during questioning. If you can't afford an attorney one will be provided for you. Do you understand these rights that I have read to you?"

"I understand, but why are you reading me my rights? I didn't do anything!"

Mike asked, "We are just covering our bases. Now, is there anything else that you can remember?"

"I don't know of anything else that I could tell you."

"That white truck that you saw, when it did get there?"

"It got there about fifteen minutes before I heard the scream, I would say about 3:15 or 3:20."

Tom asked, "When did it leave?"

"It left right after I heard the scream."

"Did you see anyone running from the house?"

"Yeah, now that you mention it."

Mike asked, "What did the person look like?"

"It was her ex."

Tom said, "Okay, tell us what your relationship with Kathy was like."

"It was just to say hi, check on the house when they were away, things like that."

"Did you pick up the mail too?"

"Yes, why do you ask?"

"Did you pick up their mail this last time that they were gone?"

"Yes, I took it to Kathy on Saturday when she got home."

Mike said, "Okay, but didn't you want to have more of a relationship with her?"

"I just wanted a friendship."

Tom asked, "Didn't you want to date her?"

"No, she was too young for me."

"Are you sure? She was very pretty. I would have wanted to be with her."

"She was refined. She would have never been with you."

"Oh, okay. Well, I can handle rejection. Can you?"

"I wasn't rejected! Is there anything else?"

Mike said, "No, you're free to go."

"Thank you."

Todd got up and walked out.

"Why did you let him go?"

"Because he was about to lawyer up, so I thought that it would be better to let him go for now and run his print against the one the crime lab has."

"You did the right thing. I was getting a little overzealous."

"I'm going to go get an evidence bag for that cup."

"I will stay here to maintain chain of custody."

Mike left to go get the bag. When he returned, he collected the cup.

"Do you want to take that to the crime lab and then head home and I'll see you in the morning."

"Are you headed home now?"

"I was going to. Do you mind?"

"It's fair you got in first today. I will see you tomorrow."

Tom walked out and headed home. As he was driving home, he was thinking that they might have found the right guy. Tom drove up to his house completely tired from his day. He walked into his house and into the kitchen.

Karen said, "Hey, you're home."

"Yes, I'm home and it's been a long day. Where are the kids?"

"The kids are upstairs taking baths. What happened today?"

"We now have a good suspect, but we have to wait for his print to come back before we will know for sure."

"Who is this guy that you think did it?"

"We think that it might be the next-door neighbor. Something just seems off about him."

"Off? What do you mean by off?"

"He just seems a little too protective of the victim."

"That would make me wonder if he had a relationship with the victim that he wasn't telling you about."

"He wasn't. She was in a relationship with her best friend. It turns out that they were a couple."

"That answers a lot of questions."

"Yeah, not to mention the best friend seems to think that there might be something there. She said that she didn't think that he would do something, but we are running out of suspects."

"I'm sure that you will figure out who did it. How was the rest of your day?"

"Well, we started out dealing with a lawyer and ended with being deceitful to get a print."

"Sounds like your kind of day."

"Yeah, but I almost tipped our hand when we were interrogating the suspect. Mike had to pull me back so that he didn't lawyer up."

"It sounds like Mike saved your case."

"Yeah, he did, just don't tell him that. What's for dinner anyways?"

"We are having spaghetti with meatballs and sausage."

"Wow, that sounds good. What made you add the sausage?"

"Just trying something different."

"Well, it sounds good. I'm looking forward to it."

"It will be ready in about ten minutes."

"Good, because I'm really hungry."

"Then why don't you set the table?"

"Did you make garlic bread?"

"Yes, why?"

"Okay, you twisted my arm."

Karen yelled, "Kids, come on, it's time for dinner."

The kids came running in to dinner. Tom and Karen brought the food to the table. Everyone sat down to eat.

Tom asked, "So how was your day, Anna?"

"My day was good. We held a spelling bee in class with the spelling words and I came in third."

"That's great. I'm proud of you."

"Thank you, Daddy."

"How was your day, Jeremy?"

"I had a good day."

"What did you do today?"

"I got to ride the tricycle today. I never get to ride it, but I did today."

"That's really exciting."

"Karen, how was your day?"

"I picked up the dry cleaning and ran some other errands. I also went to have lunch with some friends."

"Was Allison one of those friends?"

"Yes, why?"

"I was just wondering if she is looking forward to Saturday."

"Why?"

"Well, Mike is nervous about their date."

"Why is he so nervous?"

"He says that he really likes her. Is she nervous too?"

"Yes, she is. I think that she really likes him too."

"I guess that I will do the dishes if you will clear and put the food away."

"Basically, do the same thing that I always do."

"Would you rather do the dishes and I will clear and put everything away?"

"Yeah, I want to do something different."

Tom started to clear the table and Karen went over and started the dishes.

Tom said, "Kids, take your dogs outside."

The kids took the dogs outside and came back in.

Anna said, "The dogs are outside."

"Okay, honey bear. Thank you."

"Go get your spelling words so we can go over them, Anna."

"Okay, Daddy."

"I'm going to go over Anna's words with her, okay?"

"Okay. I'll go up and read with Jeremy for about 30 minutes."

"Meet on the couch?"

"I'll see you there."

Karen went upstairs to read with Jeremy. Tom went in to the living room to quiz Anna.

"Anna, are you ready?"

"Yes I am."

"Okay. Spell mailbox."

"m-a-i-l-b-o-x"

"Very good. Now spell homework."

"h-o-m-e-w-o-r-k"

"That's good, how about something?"

"s-o-m-e-t-h-i-n-g"

Tom asked her nine more words and she got all of them right.

"Now study hard, because tomorrow night we are going to go over all of them. Good job on getting them all right. I'm proud of you."

"Thank you, Daddy."

"You're welcome, princess. Now go get ready for bed. We will be up in a little bit."

"Okay, Daddy, I will."

Karen came back down the stairs to find Tom waiting for her on the couch.

"How is Jeremy doing with his reading?"

"I think that he is starting to enjoy it."

"That's really good. I'm glad that he is enjoying it. What is he reading?

"His favorite book, 'The Hungry Caterpillar.'"

"That's why he is enjoying it."

"How is Anna doing with her spelling?"

"I asked her the second half of the words tonight plus the two that she missed last night, and she got them all right."

"That's great."

"Yeah I'm so proud of her. She is really working at it."

"Well, shall we head up and put them to bed?"

"Yeah it's about that time."

Tom and Karen headed upstairs to put the kids to bed. They went to Jeremy's room first and found him playing with Blue on the floor.

"Jeremy, it's time for bed."

"Okay, Mommy."

Jeremy picked Blue up and put him into the bed. Then he climbed into bed with him and pulled up the covers. Karen bent down and kissed him on the forehead and hugged him good night.

"Good night, buddy. I love you."

"Good night Mommy. I love you too."

Tom walked over, bent down and kissed him on the forehead. Then he gave him a hug good night.

"Good night, chief. I love you."

"Good night, Daddy. I love you too."

Tom and Karen left Jeremy's room, turning off the light as they left. They then walked over to Anna's room to find her trying to get Jake to fetch.

"Okay, honey bear, it's time to get into bed."

"Okay, Mommy."

Anna picked up Jake and got into bed herself. Then she pulled up the blankets. Karen bent down and kissed her on the forehead. Then she hugged her goodnight.

"Good night, Mommy. I love you."

"Good night, honey bear. I love you too."

Tom bent down, hugged her and kissed her on the forehead good night.

"Good night, Daddy. I love you."

"Good night, princess. I love you too."

Tom and Karen walked out of Anna's room and turned off the light on the way out. They walked downstairs and collapsed on the couch.

"So how did you get to the neighbor as the one that could be the killer?"

"We went to question the best friend because with the way that she was acting she was hiding something. We decided to find out what that was."

"What was she hiding?"

"I already told you what she was hiding."

"Tell me again."

"Well, when we went to the college everyone said that they had been fighting over a guy. But that wasn't it. They were a couple and they were fighting about whether or not they wanted to come out as a couple or not."

"But how did you get to the neighbor?"

"Well, when she was going on a rant about all of this it came to her that Kathy was saying that this guy creeped her out. They didn't think that it was anything to worry about it, so she never gave it a second thought. We just thought that we should check him out."

"So, what is the hold-up now?"

"The same old story, we are waiting on prints."

"When should you get them back?"

"Hopefully tomorrow."

"So, is he just in holding until you find out?"

"No, we had to let him go. He doesn't know that we got his prints and we didn't have anything else to hold him on."

"Wonderful. Now he can get rid of evidence while you wait to find out if you can arrest him."

"No, that's the thing, Mike stopped me before I tipped our hand to him. We don't think that he thinks that we suspect him."

"So, does this mean that you're close to solving this case?"

"We have to see how the next few days play out, but we could be close because if this doesn't pan out then we are back to the best friend."

"What about an alibi for the best friend or should I say girlfriend?"

"Well, she says that she was in her room all day but there is a tree outside of her bedroom window that she could have climbed down."

"Sounds like she could have done it. Besides, didn't she find the body?"

"Yes, she did," Tom said. "I'm getting tired. Do you think that the kids have gone to sleep?"

"We can go check and go ahead and go to bed if they are."

"That sounds good to me."

Tom and Karen got up to check the doors to make sure they were locked and turned off the lights. They walked up the stairs and checked on Anna, who was sound asleep with Jake right by her side. Then they walked over to Jeremy's room to find him halfway hanging off his bed with Blue right at his back. Karen quietly walked over and pushed him back onto the bed, and Blue got up and moved to the foot.

Karen whispered, "They are so cute."

"The kids or the dogs?"

Karen smacked his arm and said, "Both."

"Come on, let's go to bed."

Tom and Karen walked into their bedroom and shut the door. They started to change clothes and Karen walked over and reached up and kissed Tom passionately. Tom kissed her back and then hugged her.

"I love you, but I am really tired tonight."

"Fine, but then you're mine on Friday night when we go on our date."

"Oh, you think that you're going to get lucky, huh?" Tom asked. "What if I don't want to put out on our first date?"

"I'm not taking no for an answer."

"I guess I'll just have to say yes then."

They climbed into bed and cuddled up together. Tom petted her hair as she fell asleep. Then he quickly fell asleep.

THURSDAY

The next morning their alarms went off and they woke up together.

Tom said, "It's morning already?"

Karen jumped out of bed.

"I should have gotten up thirty minutes ago."

She ran and got into the shower.

"I guess I'll wait."

Karen got out of the shower and walked into the room to get dressed.

"That was fast."

"I'm running late. I have to get breakfast on the table."

Karen ran downstairs while Tom got into the shower. Once he got out, he got dressed and headed downstairs.

"What's for breakfast?"

"I cut up some fruit and there are muffins on the table."

"That is a simple but good breakfast to start the day."

"I was running late today so I found something that was easy and fast."

"Well, I think that it was a good idea. Where are the kids?"

"They had better be getting up and getting dressed."

Karen ran upstairs to find Anna just coming out of her room.

Karen said, "Get downstairs. Breakfast is on the table."

"Okay, Mommy."

Karen went into Jeremy's room to find him back asleep in his bed.

"Jeremy, get up. We are running late."

Jeremy sat up and slowly got out of bed.

"You're going to have to move faster than that."

"I'm trying."

"Okay, you need to get dressed. Here are some pants and a shirt. Now get your shoes on and come downstairs."

"Okay, Mommy. I'm coming."

Karen walked back downstairs and to the breakfast table. Jeremy followed close behind.

"He was still asleep."

"Is he coming now?"

"Yes, I got him dressed and he is coming now."

"So, what does your day look like today, Anna?"

"My friend is having a birthday party in class today. Her mom is bringing cupcakes for everyone."

Karen replied, "That sounds like fun. Whose birthday is it?"

"It is Melissa's birthday today."

"Is she having a birthday party this weekend?"

"No, her family is taking a weekend trip instead."

Tom said, "Well, that sounds like fun."

"Okay, kids, we have to get going."

The kids each gave their dad a hug and Karen walked over and gave Tom a kiss goodbye. They walked out the door. Tom followed and went to work. Tom drove in and had the idea of how to get some more information on Todd Walker. He walked into the station to find Mike standing there with a cup of coffee in his hand.

"You went to Starbucks without me?"

"I got one for you too."

"Oh, you got one for me too, then you're forgiven."

Mike handed Tom a cup. Tom took the cup and took a drink.

"This is perfect. Are the prints back yet?"

"No, I called. They are running behind. They said that they should have them back this afternoon. So, what are we going to do until we get the prints back?"

"I was thinking about that. Why don't we go see the neighbor across the street from the victim? We could possibly get more information on him."

"That's an excellent idea."

"Shall we head over there now?"

"That sounds good to me."

Mike and Tom walked out to the car and drove out to head toward Gladys Baxendale's house.

"So, what information do you think that she can give us?" Mike asked.

"Well, she keeps an eye on the neighborhood and she might know more about his habits than he wants to let on."

"That's true. She can shed light on to how he treated her when he interacted with her."

"That can show us what kind of relationship he wanted with her."

"This can show a lot about him."

"That is true, this could be the whole case."

"It could certainly help a lot."

"But what kind of witness is Gladys going to be?"

"I bet that she can hold her own."

"Are you sure about that?"

"Okay, let's just talk to her and then make a judgment. We are here."

Tom and Mike walked up the path to her door. They knocked and Gladys opened the door.

Tom said, "Ms. Baxendale, I don't know if you remember us."

"Yes, I remember you, Detectives. Please call me Gladys."

Mike said, "Okay, Gladys, can we come in and talk to you for a few minutes?"

"Yes, yes, come on in."

Tom and Mike walked into the living room.

"Please have a seat."

Tom and Mike took a seat in the living room.

"Could I get you something to drink? Some coffee or tea maybe?"

"No, we are fine, thank you."

Tom asked, "Have you noticed anything out of the ordinary with your neighbor?"

"Which one?"

Mike said, "The one next door to the house directly across the street."

"Oh, the house right next to the one where the girl died?"

"That's right," Tom said.

"That was so sad. I think that he is sad too."

"Why do you say that?"

"I have noticed that he hasn't been taking care of his yard as much as he used to."

Mike asked, "How often was he in his yard working?"

"He was out there daily pruning trees and cutting his grass. He has always had the best yard in the neighborhood."

"What else does he do in his yard?"

"Well, I did see him just standing there about a month ago."

Tom asked, "What was he doing just standing there?"

"I don't know but if I didn't know any better, I would say that he was watching the dead girl in her room."

"Which room was hers?"

"Her room was the one up front overlooking the garage."

"How do you know that that was her window?"

"Because I saw him glance up there once and she was standing in view of the window."

Mike asked, "The one that you can see perfectly from his yard?"

"As a matter of fact, yes, that is the one that he was looking at. You could see into her room from his yard."

Tom asked, "Do you think that he could have been out in his yard so much because he was watching her?"

"I guess that's possible. I just never saw him as anything but harmless."

Mike said, "Yeah we have heard that before."

Tom asked, "Has he ever done anything to cause you to question his motives?"

"He has tried to talk to Kathy before, but she looked like she dismissed him."

"Did he look upset?"

"No, he looked embarrassed when he walked away."

"I'm going to ask you a direct question."

"What's that?"

"Do you think that he is a person that would kill someone?"

"Well, I wouldn't think so. But when you have lived as many years as I have you learn that people are like icebergs. They only show the tip of themselves. The rest stays hidden beneath the surface. People are always capable of doing things that most people don't think that they ever could."

"That is a profound statement."

Mike said, "I think that we have all that we need. Thank you for your time."

Tom and Mike walked out of her house and back to the car.

Mike asked, "How about we go to lunch?"

"That sounds like a good idea."

"Where do you want to go?"

"Let's go back to that diner."

"You mean Mel's Diner? We're not too far away from there."

"Yeah, that's the one."

"Okay. I could go for one of those burgers."

"That is exactly what I'm going to get."

"I think that I might try those onion rings that you are so fond of, though. We are here."

"Already? That was fast."

"I told you that we were close. Let's head in. I'm starving."

"What else is new?"

Tom and Mike walked into the diner to find that it was full. They found a table in the middle of the room. They sat down and waited for the waitress to come over. The waitress walked over looking annoyed and tired.

"Hi, my name is Molly and I will be your server today. Can I get you something to drink?"

"Are you okay?" Tom asked.

"Yeah, I'm just tired. I've been here since six this morning."

"I'm sorry. We will try to make it easy on you today. We are actually ready to order if you are."

"Awesome, what can I get you?"

"I would like a cheeseburger made with cheddar cheese and onion rings."

"What would you like to drink?"

"I would like some iced tea please."

"Okay, and for you, sir?"

Mike said, "I would like the same thing except Coke to drink and American cheese instead of cheddar."

"Very good. I will get this in for you and I will be right back with your drinks."

"Thank you."

Molly walked away to put in the order and went to get the drinks.

Mike said, "So, it sounds like Gladys would be a good witness."

"I think that she isn't a person that walks through life with rose colored glasses."

Molly returned with their drinks.

"She is really down to earth."

"I think that she would hold up to cross examination."

"She seems strong for her age."

Molly came back with their food.

"Okay, the cheeseburger with cheddar cheese for you."

She placed the burger in front of Tom.

"Here is the one with American cheese."

She placed the other burger in front of Mike.

"Is there anything else that I can get you?"

Mike said, "No, I think that is all that we need. Thank you."

Molly walked away.

Tom stated, "I think after talking to Gladys, I like Mr. Walker even more for this murder."

"Yeah, me too. I think that he is our guy."

"But still Kait seems to always point the finger at another person."

"That is true. Is she just trying to put the blame anywhere but on her?"

"I don't know, but until we get that print back, we can't rule her out."

"If Todd's print comes back and he is cleared I think that we should get hers."

"I think that is the next logical step."

Mike motioned for the waitress to come over. Molly walked over.

"Is there something that I can get you?"

"Just the check please."

"I will be right back with that."

Tom said, "I want to get back to see if that print is back."

"It will be interesting to see if he is the one."

Molly came back with the check. Mike looked at the check and it said that the total is $17.78.

Mike asked, "Are you ready?"

"Yes, I'm ready. Let's go."

Mike left a $6 tip and took the check up to the front. Then cashier walked up front.

"How was everything today?"

"Everything was great, and we had a great server."

"Who was your server?"

"Her name was Molly, and she is great."

"I will let management know that you had a good experience with her. You total is $17.78."

Mike handed her a 20.

"Can you make sure that she gets the change please?"

"Yes, I will. Have a good day."

"You too."

Tom and Mike walked out to the car and headed down the road to the station.

Tom said, "I'll bet you that Todd's print comes back as a match."

"What do you want to bet?"

"That was rhetorical, but okay, if I win you have to babysit again next weekend too."

"So, I will have to babysit two weekends in a row?"

"Yes. That's fair."

"Fine then. If I win then you have to find a new babysitter this week."

"It's a bet. But you know I'm going to win."

"I think that you will win too."

"That print should be back by the time that we get back to the station."

"I hope so. We have waited long enough. Their backlog shouldn't take this long. Things have been quiet lately."

"Don't jinx us. We don't want things to get busy."

"True."

Tom and Mike pulled into the driveway of the police station and parked their car. They walked in to find the bullpen busy. People were everywhere, walking around and all the interrogation rooms were filled.

"See what you did? You jinxed us."

"I didn't do this," Mike replied. "I'll bet this was already like this before I said anything."

"Maybe so, but I'm going to blame you anyways."

Mike chuckled a little.

"Of course, you are."

Mike walked over to his desk to find a manila envelope. He picked it und opened it.

"What is that? Is that what I think that it is?"

"Yes, we are about to find out who won the bet. Did I get out of Friday night or am I busy for the next two weekends?"

"Oh, come on. Just open it."

Mike looked at the report.

"Okay, I'm torn."

"Why?"

"Because am I happy that we found the killer or am I sad that I'm busy for the next two weekends?"

"That's great news. You are happy. Trust me, you're happy."

"I guess. Now we have to put in for the search warrant."

"Can't we just go and arrest him?"

"You know that we can't if you want whatever we find in his house to be admissible in court."

"I know," Tom replied. "I just wish that we could go do it now."

"We will just give him one more day of freedom."

"Yeah, one more day of thinking that he got away with it."

"Who gets to fill out the paperwork for the warrant? Not it!"

"Not it! Damn it. Well, I guess I get to do that. But I want your input."

"Of course."

"Let me get out the paperwork. Okay, the reason that we want the warrant."

"Because he is guilty."

"That's not helping. Because his fingerprint was on the murder weapon. Okay, what do we want to search?"

"Make sure that it includes the whole house."

Tom said, "And his car."

"Don't forget the surrounding land around his house to include his backyard."

"That's a good idea. Now what are we looking for?"

"Make sure to include clothing items."

"Including shoes."

"That's a good idea. What about pictures which would show an interest or obsession with her?"

"That's good but we need to include camera equipment as well as his phone."

"Don't forget his computer and any storage devices."

"We should look for letters that he wrote or a journal or something else like that."

"We should also look to see if he has had someone that he obsessed over before."

"I think that is it. I hope that we get this back by tomorrow."

"With the evidence that we already have it shouldn't take too long, don't you think?"

"I think that it will be back right away," Tom replied. "If we could have put in for this morning, then we would have probably been able to serve it today."

"Yeah, but it's getting late. Since you filled it out, I will drop it off. I will see you in the morning."

"Okay, good night."

Tom drove home thinking about how lucky he was to have his family and friends that he could count on. He thought that he loved his wife so much and he couldn't stand to think about what would happen if something were to happen to her. How lost he would be. He drove up to his house just thankful that he had a family to go home to. Tom walked into the house to find Karen in the same place as every time when he got home: cooking in the kitchen. Tom walked over and placed his hands around her back and gave her a passionate kiss.

"What is that for?"

"Just because I love you."

"I love you too. Welcome home."

"Thank you. What's for dinner?"

"Tonight, I have a real treat for you. I'm making home-made lasagna."

"Wow, we haven't had that in a while. I came home to two things that I love, one more than the other. Don't feel bad. I have known lasagna longer."

"Hey! You don't mean that."

"You know that I don't. I was just trying to be funny. What made you make lasagna?"

"I was feeling ambitious today."

"Well, I welcome it."

"I thought that you would."

"Where are the kids?"

"They are upstairs playing."

"Don't they have homework?"

"Their teachers let them off easy tonight. Jeremy doesn't have any homework and Anna only has to study for her spelling test for tomorrow and she does that with you, so I told them that they could play until dinner."

"That sounds reasonable."

"I thought so. So how was work? Did you catch the guy yet?"

"Funny that you should ask that."

"Did you?"

"Not yet, but we now know who did it."

"Really, who?"

"It was the neighbor next door."

"Really. Why?"

"We don't really know yet, but we are hoping to find out tomorrow when we arrest him."

"Why are you waiting until tomorrow?"

"Because we are waiting for the warrant to come back."

"But if you know who did it, why do you need a warrant?"

"Because without a warrant everything that we found at his house would be inadmissible in court."

"If you need to look for evidence then how do you know that it was him?"

"Because we have his fingerprint."

"If you have his fingerprint then why do you need more evidence?"

"Because it makes our case stronger and then he won't slip away and get away with murder. We like to giftwrap the killer for the DA so that the case is a slam dunk."

"Oh, I see. Your job can be frustrating. You know who the guy is, but you can't go and arrest him because of bureaucracy."

"That sounds about right. We want to build the best case that we can because we only get one shot at proving his guilt."

Karen yelled, "Kids, dinner is ready!"

The kids came running down the stairs and into the kitchen.

Karen asked, "Did you two wash your hands?"

Anna said, "Oops, I forgot."

"Then I suggest that you go get your hands washed."

"Me too?"

"Yes, you too."

The kids went to the bathroom and washed their hands. They came back out and sat down at the table.

"Honey, could you carry over the lasagna pan and I will get the salad and the bread."

"Okay, I got it."

Tom walked over to get the lasagna and took it to the table. They all sat down at the table. Tom started to cut the lasagna and gave each person a piece.

Tom asked, "Anna, how was the birthday party today?"

"It was so much fun. We had chocolate cupcakes."

Karen replied, "Wow, that's awesome. That is your favorite."

"Yeah."

Tom asked, "How was the rest of your day?"

"It was fine. My teacher didn't give us any homework. She said that it was a birthday present for Melissa."

"That's cool. But you do still have to study your spelling words tonight."

"I know, but I don't have to do anything else."

"Jeremy, how was your day?"

"I had a good day."

Karen asked, "What happened today that made it good?"

"My class started this thing where if you get caught doing something good, they put your name in a bowl for a drawing at the end of the month and the winner gets a prize."

"That's a good program. When did that start?"

"This month."

Tom asked, "So did you get your name in the bowl?"

"Yes."

"What did you do to get put into the bowl?" Karen asked.

"I found broken glass on the playground and pointed it out to the playground monitor."

Karen said, "That is a good thing. I'm proud of you."

Tom said, "Wow, that was a good dinner. It really hit the spot."

"Thank you. Now we have to clean up the mess."

"Do you want to clear and put away or do the dishes?"

"I want to clear and put away."

"Okay, I will start the dishes then."

Tom and Karen got up and started to clean up the kitchen.

"Kids, take your dogs outside."

Anna said, "Okay, Daddy."

"How soon do you think you will get the warrant back?"

"We are hoping to get it back approved tomorrow morning."

"You mean it might not be approved?"

"It depends on the judge. If he is a judge that wants to cover himself, then he might require more for the warrant. But I don't see there being a problem."

Anna said, "The dogs are outside."

Tom said, "Thank you. Now go get your pajamas on."

"Okay, I will."

"Jeremy, get yours on too."

"Okay, Mommy."

"So, what was your day like today?"

"My day was great. I spent the day cleaning, doing laundry, things like that. You know what I do on Thursdays."

"I'm sorry. Is there anything that I can do for you this evening?"

"How about after I read with Jeremy you massage my feet?"

"I will do as you wish."

"In that case I might need to abuse that privilege."

"Now wait a minute."

"Relax, I'm just kidding. All I need is the foot massage."

"Okay, in that case yes I will give you a foot massage when you come down from reading with Jeremy."

"Speaking of which, I need to get up there."

"I need to get going on Anna's spelling words too."

Karen went upstairs to read with Jeremy.

Tom yelled, "Anna, come down here with your spelling list."

Anna came running down the stairs, passing her mom on the way.

"Slow down."

"Sorry, Mommy."

"Let me see your list."

Anna handed her dad the list of words.

"Are you ready?"

"Yes I am."

"Okay, spell raincoat."

"r-a-i-n-c-o-a-t"

"Very good. Spell snowman."

"s-n-o-w-m-a-n"

"Good job. Spell cupcake."

"c-u-p-c-a-k-e"

"That's good."

Tom and Anna went over seventeen more words and she got all the words right.

"You're doing a great job. Just do like you did tonight and you will be fine. Go ahead and head upstairs to brush your teeth and get ready for bed."

"Okay, Daddy."

Karen came back downstairs and collapsed on the opposite side of the couch from Tom and put her feet in his lap. Tom immediately picked up her left foot and started to rub it.

"That feels so good."

"I'm here to please."

"How did Anna do with her quiz that you gave her?"

"She got every word right. If she does that on the test, then she will have her A."

Tom picked up Karen's right foot and started to rub it.

"That is great."

"How is Jeremy doing with his reading?"

"Jeremy said tonight that he is having fun when he is reading with me."

"Sweetie, that is really good."

"I guess it's time to go put these kids to bed."

They walked upstairs and went into Jeremy's room first. When they stepped in, they found Blue lying on the bed and Jeremy playing with his cars on the floor.

"Come on, chief, it's time for bed."

"Okay, Daddy."

He climbed into bed and pulled the blankets up. Tom leaned down and gave him a kiss on the forehead and hugged him good night.

"Good night, chief. I love you."

"Good night, Daddy. I love you too."

Karen walked over and bent down, kissed him on the forehead and hugged him good night.

"Good night, buddy. I love you."

"Good night, Mommy. I love you too."

They then walked over to Anna's room and found her playing tug of war with Jake.

"Goodnight, honey bear. I love you."

"Good night, Mommy. I love you too."

Tom walked over, leaned down and gave her a kiss on the forehead and hugged her good night.

"Good night, Daddy. I love you."

"Good night, princess. I love you too."

Tom and Karen walked back downstairs and over to the couch. They sat back down and cuddled up together.

Tom asked, "What do you want to watch tonight?"

"It doesn't matter to me. Whatever you want to watch."

Tom turned on the TV and they sat and watched as they both fell asleep together on the couch. Tom woke up a few hours later and woke up Karen.

"Karen, Karen, wake up."

"What?"

"It's around 11 o'clock. We need to get to bed."

"Okay, I'm up. I want to check on the kids on the way to bed."

They shut down all the lights and locked the doors. Then they went upstairs and walked over to Anna's room. Anna was sound asleep on her bed. Karen walked over and pulled her blankets back up. Then they walked over to Jeremy's room and found him flat on his back with Blue's head on his chest.

"They are so cute."

"When they are sleeping."

Karen cracked a smile and smacked Tom on the arm.

"Come on, let's go to bed."

Tom and Karen walked into their room and shut the door. As they changed clothes, Karen walked over and kissed Tom.

"Just remember, tomorrow night you're mine."

"Should I be scared?"

"What do you think?"

"That's it. I'm scared."

They climbed into bed and cuddled up together.

"You should be."

They kissed each other good night and Tom petted Karen's head until she fell asleep. Then he drifted off to sleep.

FRIDAY

The next morning Tom woke up and found Karen had already gotten up. He took his shower and went downstairs. Karen was cooking in the kitchen.

"Come on, kids, it's time for breakfast. Oh, good morning, honey. Come on, let's eat."

"No, I'll get something later. I want to find out about that warrant."

"You can wait ten minutes. That's enough time for you to eat."

"Okay, what are we having?"

"Eggs, bacon, and toast."

"Bacon? Okay, I will stay if you insist."

The kids came in and they all sat down at the table to eat.

Tom asked, "Anna, are you ready for your test?"

"I'm as ready as I will ever be."

"That's good."

Karen asked, "Jeremy, when is that drawing?"

"It's the last school day of the month."

"Well, that's only two weeks away."

"I know. I'm going to try to get my name in the bowl again today."

"What are your plans, sweetie?"

"I don't know, I was thinking about going shopping with Allison after she gets done this morning."

"Doesn't she have class?"

"No, she is off on Fridays, so all she has is before school and after school. She is coming here when she gets off this morning."

"What is this going to cost us?"

"I'll keep it reasonable, but she wants to get something for tomorrow night with Mike. Come on, kids, it's time to go to school. Give your dad a hug goodbye."

The kids each came over and hugged their dad goodbye for the day and Karen came over and kissed him.

"I can't wait for tonight."

"Me either. Have a good day, everyone. Anna, good luck on your test today."

"Thank you, Daddy."

Tom got up and headed off to work. He was hoping that the warrant would be back so that they could go arrest Todd for Kathy's murder. When Tom got into work he walked inside and found Mike sitting at his desk.

"Is the warrant back yet?"

"I don't know but there is an envelope sitting on your desk."

"You didn't open it?"

"It's not mine."

Tom walked over and opened the envelope to find that it was the warrant approved and signed.

"Are we a go?"

"Yes, we are a go. Do we have some uniforms ready to go with us?"

"Yes, they are standing by."

"Then let's head over there."

Tom and Mike walked out of the door and drove over to Todd Walker's house.

"What do you think that we will find when we get there?" Mike asked.

"I think that we will find a scared man. I don't think that he will fight us at all."

"What do you think that we need to look for? I mean, we already have the murder weapon."

"We need to find anything that puts him with the body because he could say that he went in and touched the knife after she was dead."

"And didn't report it?"

"Yes, he could have gotten scared."

"You should be a defense lawyer. You would be good at it."

"Thanks a lot, but I will use my power for good. We need to be looking for clothes with blood splatter on them."

"Well, let's head in."

Tom and Mike walked with about four police officers up to the door of Todd Walker. Tom knocked on the door and Todd opened it.

"Can I help you?"

Tom replied, "Yes, you can step outside."

"Why?"

"Because we have a search warrant for your home, car and yard."

"I'm not going to allow that."

Mike responded, "You don't have a choice. You are under arrest for the murder of Kathy Jefferson."

"That's insane. I would never do that."

"You have the right to be silent. Anything that you say can and will be used against you in a court of law. You have the right to an attorney and to have one present during questioning. If you can't afford an attorney one will be provided for you. Do you understand these rights that I have read to you?"

"Yes, I do. But I don't understand why you're arresting me."

Mike escorted Todd to the police car and put him into the backseat. Then he rejoined the search.

Mike asked, "Have we found anything?"

"Not yet, but we just started looking."

Just then an officer walked out for the bedroom.

"You've got to see this."

Tom and Mike walked back to the bedroom and saw in the closet a wall full of pictures of Kathy. Some were of her in the backyard lying out sunbathing in a swimsuit. Some were of her in the front yard and the rest were of her in the window of her bedroom. All were taken from his yard. She appeared to be unaware of them being taken. Then Mike looked down and saw some white tennis shoes with a small drop of dark red on them.

Mike said, "Bag these. There is some blood on them."

"Did you notice the fire pit in the back yard?"

"What are you getting at?"

"He might have burned his clothes to hide the blood. I'm going to go out there and look."

Tom walked out to the fire pit and looked through the ashes. Then a piece of charred blue denim caught his eye. His used his gloved hand and picked it up. The edges of it were burned but the middle was untouched and there was blood on it.

"Mike, come check this out."

Mike came out and asked, "What is that?"

"It is a piece of blue jeans that didn't burn when he tried to destroy the evidence and there is blood on it."

"What is the difference between the cleaned tennis shoes and the burned pants?"

"Well, he could have just been there got some blood on his shoes after the murder and he cleaned them. Burning the clothes shows that he is trying to cover something up. I think that we have enough to possibly get a confession so let's let them finish up here and we can go talk to him at the station."

Mike went to the officer that drove the car that Todd was in.

"Hey, head back to the station with him and put him in the box."

Tom and Mike walked out, got in the car and headed back to the station.

Mike asked, "Do you want to get something to eat before heading back to the station?"

"That might be a good idea. It might be a long afternoon."

"Where do you want to go?"

"I was thinking that we could go back to Ming Palace."

"That's a good idea. I could go for some Chinese food."

"Let's head over there."

They got to Ming Palace and parked a few spaces down. They walked into the restaurant to find that they were early for the lunch rush. They had the whole restaurant to choose a place to sit.

"Sit anywhere that you like, gentlemen."

Tom asked, "Where do you want to sit?"

"Let's sit over here by the window."

They sat down by the front window just away from the door. The waitress walked out, and it was someone familiar. Jiayi walked over.

"My name is Jiayi, I will be serving you today. Wait, don't I know you guys?"

"Yes, you do," Tom said. "We were in here…"

"Last week, I remember. How are you doing today?"

"We are doing good. How is your day going?"

"My day is good. What can I get you today?"

"Well, I want orange chicken with fried rice and an iced tea to drink."

Mike said, "I would like sesame chicken with fried rice and a Coke."

"Okay, I will get that order in right away."

"How do you think that he is going to react when we get in there to talk to him?"

"Well, I think that he is going to be confrontational because we kept him waiting."

Jiayi walked back over with their drinks.

"Here you go."

Mike said, "Thank you."

"You're welcome. Your lunch will be right out."

Jiayi walked back to the back of the restaurant.

Mike asked, "Do you think that we will get a confession?"

"I think that he is going to be dying to explain himself."

"He will probably give himself away then."

"Yeah, I would go with that."

Jiayi walked back over with two plates and a large bowl of fried rice.

"Is there anything else that I can get for you two?"

Mike said, "No, I think that will do it for now."

Jiayi walked away, flashing a smile at Tom as she left.

"She has a crush on you."

"No, she doesn't. She is just trying to get a bigger tip."

"I don't think so. She smiled at you the last time that we were in here as well."

"I'm married, and I wear a ring."

"I don't think that she cares."

"Shut up and eat your chicken."

When they were done eating, Tom motioned Jiayi over.

"What can I get for you?"

"We just need the check please."

"I will get that right away for you."

Jiayi walked away to the register and started working up the check.

"I'll bet that she is writing down her number for you."

"Shut up, she is not."

Jiayi walked back over and put the check face down, looked Tom right in the eye.

"Call me sometime."

She then walked away. Tom looked down at the check and saw that there was her name and a phone number written on the back of the check.

"See? I told you."

"Shut up."

"What are you going to do?"

"I'm going to let her down easy."

Tom wrote on the back of the check. Then turned it over to see the total. The total was $33.62. Tom pulled out $45 and took it up to Jiayi.

"I'm sorry, keep the change."

Jiayi turned the check over and Tom had written I'm sorry, I'm happily married. Tom and Mike walked out of the restaurant and headed back to the station.

Mike asked, "So what is our strategy in getting him to talk when we get in there?"

"We need to gain rapport with him. We need him to think that he was justified in his actions."

"Are you sure that we shouldn't just go at him?"

"We will after we have him talking."

"How do we build rapport with him?"

"We talk to him about how attractive Kathy was, things like that."

"I just want this case over and finished."

"I know what you mean. I'm tired of losing sleep over this one. I hate when they are so senseless like this was."

"Yeah. When people commit murder, it doesn't make sense but at least there is a logic behind it. It may be twisted but it is still there."

"You're right. When someone kills because they in some twisted way love the person it doesn't make since."

"Well, let's go in and see where we are at with him."

Tom and Mike drove into the driveway and parked. Then they walked into the station and back to the interrogation room. They observed him for a few minutes to see how he was reacting to being arrested. Todd was nervous. He was pacing back and forth. The officer that brought him in had brought him something to eat in a brown bag and he didn't even touch it. He didn't even open the bag. Tom and Mike walked into the room.

"I don't know why I am here."

Tom replied, "We are just going to talk for a few minutes."

"What about?"

"We just want to talk about Kathy Jefferson."

"Why did I get arrested for her murder?"

"Let's talk about something else first."

Mike asked, "What kind of relationship did you want with her?"

"We were friends."

"I didn't ask what your relationship was like. I asked what relationship you wanted?"

"I didn't want anything more than that."

Tom asked, "Are you sure?"

"Yes why?"

"Well, because she was a beautiful woman."

"So?"

Mike said, "We also found all the pictures that you took without her knowledge on your closet wall."

"She let me take those pictures."

Tom asked, "Oh? Did she let you into her house to kill her too?"

"I didn't kill her!"

"Then why did we find blood splatter on your shoes?" Mike replied. "You cleaned them mostly, but some was still there."

"I cut myself so that is my blood."

Tom said, "You know that we are going to run DNA testing on it."

"Go ahead."

"What about the charred clothing in the back yard? Oh, and neither blood type is yours. It is the same as Kathy's though."

"Fine! I did it, I killed her! But she just made me so angry."

Mike asked, "What did she do?"

"I kissed her, and she pushed me away. Who is she to reject me?"

Tom said, "Okay. Here is some paper and a pen. We need you to write down what happened."

The door opened, and an officer poked his head into the room.

"Tom, they are here."

"Okay. I will be right out."

"I've got this. Go ahead."

Tom walked out of the room.

"They are in the interview room over there."

"Okay. Thank you."

Tom walked into the interview room and sat down with Paul and Susan Jefferson.

Paul asked, "Do you have an update for us?"

"Yes, I do. Apparently, your neighbor Todd Walker is the one who killed her."

Susan responded, "Oh my God, we have always had him pick up our mail when we went out of town. I would have never thought."

"Yeah, Kathy's girlfriend said the same thing."

Paul said, "You mean best friend."

"No, I don't. Well, he saw that she came home on Saturday and on Sunday he took the mail over to her. Then when she had her back turned, he walked closer to her and when she turned around, he kissed her. She pushed him away. He asked her what was wrong, and she said that she didn't like him that way and she said that he was too old for her. Then he grabbed a knife from the butcher block and stabbed her in the abdomen and when he saw what he did he then decided that he needed to kill her if he wanted to get away with it. So, he stabbed her in the heart."

Susan was crying, and Paul had tears in his eyes.

"I hope that it helps to know what had happened."

"I'm not sure anything can help."

"I think that with some counseling you will be okay. It just takes time."

"I know. This guy is going to prison?"

"Yes, he confessed to it. He will be going away for a long time."

"We would like to invite you to the funeral tomorrow at noon," Susan said. "I hope that both you and Detective Turner can make it."

"We will be there."

Paul and Susan stood up and walked out of the room just as Todd was being escorted to holding.

"How could you! She was my baby. You're sick. I hope that you die in prison."

Paul put his arms around her, and they walked out of the station. As Tom watched the doors close behind them, he thought, I hope they will be okay and get through this.

HERZ FÜR AUTOREN A HEART FOR AUTHORS À L'ÉCOUTE DES AUTEURS MIA ΚΑΡΔΙΑ ΓΙΑ ΣΥΤΡΑ
FÖR FÖRFATTARE UN CORAZÓN POR LOS AUTORES YAZARLARIMIZA GÖNÜL VERELIM SZÍV
PER AUTORI ET HJERTE FOR FORFATTERE EEN HART VOOR SCHRIJVERS TEMOS OS AUTOR
ZOINKÉRT SERCE DLA AUTORÓW EIN HERZ FÜR AUTOREN A HEART FOR AUTHORS À L'ÉCOUTI
ВСЕЙ ДУШОЙ К АВТОРАМ ETT HJÄRTA FÖR FÖRFATTARE À LA ESCUCHA DE LOS AUTORI
MIA ΚΑΡΔΙΑ ΓΙΑ ΣΥΤΡΑΦΕΙΣ UN CUORE PER AUTORI ET HJERTE FOR FORFATTERE EEN Η
YAZARLARIMIZA ZOINKÉRT SERCE DLA AUTORÓW EIN HERZ FÜR
SCHRIJVERS CO AÇÃO ВСЕЙ ДУШОЙ К АВТОРАМ ETT HJÄRTA FÖR

The author

Gregory Sallee was born in San Bernardino, California. After high school he became a truck driver before joining the army. He met and married his wife toward the end of his military career and they had a son together. After attaining the rank of sergeant, he left the army. He went back to truck driving. He stopped driving when an illness caught up to him from his time in Iraq causing problems with his lungs. He lost his wife at the age of 40 and, wanting to do something meaningful, he began writing. His favorite activities are being in nature, watching movies, and spending time with family and friends. He loves coming up with stories and sharing them with anyone who wants to read them.

The publisher

He who stops getting better stops being good.

This is the motto of novum publishing, and our focus is on finding new manuscripts, publishing them and offering long-term support to the authors.
Our publishing house was founded in 1997, and since then it has become THE expert for new authors and has won numerous awards.

Our editorial team will peruse each manuscript within a few weeks free of charge and without obligation.

You will find more information about
novum publishing and our books on the internet:

www.novumpublishing.com

CPSIA information can be obtained
at www.ICGtesting.com
Printed in the USA
LVHW112019120520
655429LV00012B/181